HER NOBLE HIGHLANDER

ALSO BY JENNAE VALE

THE THISTLE & HIVE SERIES

A Bridge Through Time - Book 1

A Thistle Beyond Time - Book 2

Separated by Time - Book 3

A Matter of Time - Book 4

A Thistle & Hive Christmas - Book 4.5

A Turn in Time - Book 5

All In Good Time - Book 6

A Long Forgotten Time - Book 7

THE MACKALLS OF DUNNET HEAD

Her Trusted Highlander - Book 1

A HIGHLANDER IN VEGAS

HER NOBLE HIGHLANDER

THE MACKALLS OF DUNNET HEAD

JENNAE VALE

CHAPTER 1

HIDDEN IN THE shadows of the darkened alley, Pierce Holmes waited and watched. He had been following this small family for weeks, waiting for his opportunity. His nerves were getting the better of him as they had every time thus far. Never having done this before, he wasn't sure he wanted to do it now. He shifted his weight from foot to foot, as his eyes skimmed over the alley and the street. It was Sunday morning and there was no one else around. This was the opportune time he'd been waiting for. He could grab the child and make a run for it, but first he'd have to subdue the mother and father, not permanently of course, but just long enough to get the girl and disappear.

This should be easy, but something was holding him back. A presence. He wasn't alone. Someone was watching him. He gazed up at the windows of the surrounding buildings, but saw no one. Pinned up against the wall of the alley, he turned his head from side to side, quickly assessed the situation. No matter how hard he looked, there was no one in sight. His gut told him this wasn't going to work, even though it had seemed perfect only moments ago. He cursed silently to himself. This would not be the day. He would not take the first step on his journey towards great wealth and revenge. He'd wait.

Despite the gnawing need in his head to complete his mission, the feeling that someone knew what he was up to wouldn't leave him. His brain was battling his gut on this one. Ever since he'd found those papers in Malcolm Granger's office he'd been a man possessed. All he could think about was getting his hands on the Twin Sword. He'd thought Malcolm crazy when he'd dragged them through time to retrieve it. Oddly, he'd forgotten all about it until he found the papers. Since that moment he could think of nothing but possessing the sword. He had flown halfway around the world to ensure it would be his. All he needed was the child.

Now, here he stood in an alley in Edinburgh, ready to pounce on the unsuspecting couple, but something was holding him back. Perhaps it was his own uneasiness over his plan or perhaps this unseen watcher was real. It couldn't be. He had been so careful. No one knew of his plans, no one knew where he was. He balled his fists and growled at his own cowardice. The woman pushing the pram glanced in his direction. Whether she saw him or not, he couldn't say, but she did hurry her steps as her husband followed along beside her.

"WHAT'S WRONG, LOVE?" David Sinclair asked his wife.

"I'm nae sure. I keep having this feeling that someone is following us." Maureen Sinclair warily glanced back over her shoulder. "I thought I heard a growl."

David looked back and scanned the area. It all looked perfectly normal, she knew, just a few shoppers out enjoying a Saturday afternoon. "I didn't see any dogs," he assured her.

"I don't think it was a dog. It sounded like a man." She shivered at the thought.

"I'm sure it was nothing. Probably only a drunken sot asleep in that alley over there." He glanced back over his shoulder and paused to stare at some movement in the alley. He stared for a moment, his brow furrowed, then turned and placed his hand on her back to hurry them along. "We should get home. It looks like it might rain."

"David, this isn't the first time I've had this feeling." She'd experienced this before. Over the last two weeks she frequently felt uneasy when out with Molly. She peered around the aisles at the grocery store trying to catch whoever was watching. She had stopped going to the park completely because it just didn't feel safe there anymore. It was ridiculous, she thought, but she needed to tell David. Maybe he could help her see it was all in her imagination. "It scares me."

He stopped and looked into her eyes. "I won't let anything happen to you or Molly." He wrapped his arms around her and his warmth pushed some of the fear away. He kissed her head and stepped back from her, "I'll go back and take a look. See who's there." He turned back towards the alley, but Maureen grabbed his arm.

"No!" She knew she sounded frantic, but her mother's intuition was telling her that whoever had been following them wanted little Molly.

"Are you sure?" David turned back to her, worry etching his brow.

"Aye. I'm sure." She was afraid. What if something happened to David? What if whoever was watching them harmed him in such a way that it would be easy to take Molly. She had to get these thoughts out of her head. The many uneasy nights without sleep and days of worry gave her a constant headache. She could hardly concentrate on her work in the bakery. Yesterday she burned an entire pan of scones and twice gave customers the wrong change. If only she could prove to herself that it was all in her imagination. But what if she couldn't prove it? What if it was true? Then she'd be even more terrified. This was her wee bairn. She couldn't allow anything to happen to her. If it did, her life would be over. One thing she knew for sure, she would do whatever she had to do in order to protect wee Molly.

They hurried back to their little apartment above the bakery, entering through the door that led upstairs just as the first drops of rain began to fall.

"Ye made it back just in time," Mrs. May said, surprising them so that they both jumped. "I'm sorry. I didnae mean to scare ye."

Maureen took a deep breath, trying to calm her pounding heart. "'Tis fine. We werenae expecting to run into ye, 'tis all."

Mrs. May laughed, her blue eyes twinkling with warmth. It was apparent she didn't realize how terrified Maureen had been. She crouched down to Molly's level, "And how is our Miss Molly doing today? Did you have a lovely time out with mum and da?"

Molly's face lit with a smile, her pudgy little finger pointing to the bakery entrance.

"Oh, she's a precious one, our Molly." Mrs. May sprang up, patting her mop of grey hair back into place and turning to Maureen. She was quite spry for a lady over sixty, must be the decades of bending and mixing. "I'm on me way back to the bakery. I left Mr. May to tend the customers. I hope he hasnae scared them all away." She chuckled and squeezed past them. "I left some shortbread for ye, by yer door."

"'Tis verra kind of ye. Many thanks," David said.

"Think nothing of it." She smiled warmly at them, softly caressing Molly's cheek before disappearing through the door that led from their apartments into the bakery.

Maureen relaxed enough to laugh as she heard Mrs. May berating her husband through the closed door.

"She's quite the character, that one," David said. He picked wee Molly out of the pram, which Maureen then parked under the stairs.

"I'll be happy to be back in our cozy little home," Maureen said, following him up the stairs past Peter and Ethel May's second floor apartment just above the bakery, to the third-floor flat they had rented shortly after getting married. They really needed to move to a bigger place, preferably one where there was no stair climbing involved. It would have to wait though. David's salary from his job at the bank, barely covered their expenses and the money Maureen made working part time in the bakery all went into their savings. It would take some time, but eventually they'd be able to afford their own small cottage. It was their goal and one they both were

4

working hard to attain.

David picked up the shortbread. "Mmm…"

"I'll make some tea as soon as I put Molly down for a nap. Are ye tired, love?" she asked as she watched her daughter yawning and rubbing her eyes. "Come. Let's have a wee lie down." Maureen took her from her Da.

They'd reached the safety of their home. Maureen could feel the tension leaving her as soon as the door closed. She looked around the little family room at the comfortable couch where she and David watched movies at night, at the pile of toys Molly played with during the day, at the photos of family and friends along the mantle and felt lighter. They were together and her little family was fine. She'd put her fear aside for the time being and concentrate on what was right in front of her instead of the unknown.

"I'll put the water on," David said, already munching on a piece of shortbread.

"I'll be right back. Dinnae eat it all," she teased, raising an eyebrow at her husband.

He smiled broadly and continued munching away as she disappeared into her wee daughter's room.

CHAPTER 2

"Maggie… Dylan… I must speak with ye," Edna Campbell said as she marched into the dining room.

Maggie sat at one of the tables with receipts spread around her laptop. She looked up at Edna as Dylan poked his head out from the kitchen and the wonderful smell of beef bourguignon wafted into the room, "Is something wrong?" he asked.

"Nae. Well, aye." Edna hesitated for a moment before continuing. "Not here in Glendaloch."

Dylan came into the room and stood behind Maggie. "What's wrong?" Dylan asked again.

"Dylan, did ye ken ye have family in Edinburgh?" she asked.

He appeared thoughtful for a moment and then shook his head. "No. I do?"

"Aye. Distant cousins." Edna said. She paced back and forth between the tables deep in thought, then nodded determinedly and sat down. Dylan took the seat beside his wife and reached for Maggie's hand.

The two didn't say a word, waiting for Edna to continue.

"There's trouble there. I saw it today."

"What kind of trouble?" Maggie asked.

"Anania, the Elven Queen, has been in touch with me about a man." She gazed out the window and fell silent, her mind wandering to her conversation with Anania. There was a great deal to consider. They must keep the bairn safe. The evil was locked away, but for how long?

"Auntie, what man? What trouble?" It was obvious Maggie was losing patience with Edna.

"I'm sorry." Edna shook her head and refocused on her family. "I've much going on in me head. Yer cousins are Maureen and David Sinclair. They have a child named Molly. She's a precious wee one. Not even two years old. This man wishes to take her from them."

"Oh, no!" Maggie said, bolting up from her chair and almost knocking it over as she did. "We have to help them."

"Why do we have to help them?" Both women shot him a look and he raised his hands in defense. "I mean, of course we should, but are we the best people to help? Shouldn't they call the police?" Dylan asked.

"Under normal circumstances they would, but in this case there is magic and evil involved." She gazed at Dylan, worrying that perhaps it wasn't the best idea to send him. What if some harm befell him? He couldn't protect himself the way a witch could. "On second thought, Maggie I believe ye should go alone."

"Absolutely not!" Dylan firmly stated. "I'm going with her and I'm not going to argue with you about it."

Edna loved Dylan. He was a good lad and she was happy he loved Maggie so much. "Alright. I trust that Maggie can protect ye." She noted Dylan's raised eyebrow and crossed arms. "And that ye can protect Maggie."

Dylan relaxed his stance. "What do we need to do?"

"Ye must go to Edinburgh and introduce yerself to the Sinclairs."

"Won't that be weird? I've never heard of them until just now. I'm sure they don't know who I am either." His eyebrows were knitted together.

"Weird it may be, but it is of the utmost importance. Ye must convince them to allow me to send their Molly back in time to your many times great grandfather, Aleck Sinclair. He will protect the child until we can take care of the man who's after her."

"You want me to convince them to send their child back in time? Edna this is crazy, even for you." Dylan shook his head in disbelief.

7

Edna looked Dylan in the eye, her voice firm and sure, "I ken it willnae be easy, but he could take the child at any moment and I believe her life is in danger. Ye must trust me, Dylan. The existence of the Sinclair name is at stake." Dylan's eye's widened as the severity of the situation settled on his shoulders.

"How is that possible?" he whispered.

"If this man manages to get his hands on Molly, he'll need her blood, along with an emerald gem to open the vault where the Twin Sword is located. He wishes to possess it as much as Malcolm Granger once did. Ariweth is influencing his thoughts and actions." Edna stood and resumed her pacing. This was no ordinary evil. "Anania was forced to increase her spell on the vault, so he cannot control him completely. We must protect the little girl and find a way to break the hold he has over this man. We can not allow that vault to be opened. The last thing this world needs is for that wicked sorcerer to be set free along with the sword."

"I don't understand. How is the blood of Molly Sinclair what he needs to open the vault?" Edna could see that Maggie was trying desperately to put this all together.

"I ken I'm nae doing a good job of telling ye what ye must understand." Edna paced back and forth, trying to put her thoughts into words that would make sense. Everything she'd told them so far was coming out in the wrong order. It must seem completely nonsensical to them, but there was so much to do. She needed them to understand the importance of keeping Molly safe, but she knew she could not tell them everything. She could not let them know the consequences of failing would be dire for everyone.

Dylan, in his typical laid-back fashion, went to Edna and placed a calming hand on her shoulder. "We'll go. This must be important for you to even ask. Besides, I've been wanting to see Edinburg."

Edna visibly relaxed. This plan would work. "Thank ye, my dear. 'Tis for ye and all yer family that this must be done. Now, once you are there, I want you to befriend the young couple. I don't want them so frightened that they try to run away. That would make it difficult for us to help."

"When do you want us to leave?" Dylan asked.

"As soon as ye can get packed," she responded.

"Will ye be joining us, Auntie?" Maggie asked.

"Nae. I cannae." Edna said.

"Aye. Right. I forgot the bridge." Maggie joined Dylan at Edna's side. "Come love, we should pack."

"I'll be here to help in any way that I can," Edna assured them.

Alone with her thoughts, Edna tried to piece together the information she'd received from Anania. Who could this man be? How did he know about the Twin Sword? It was only a legend in this time. Not many believed that it actually existed, but she knew that it did and she also knew the problems that would arise if this man got his hands on it. Not long ago she'd fought another who lusted after the sword. She'd turned him to stone and buried him in the rock vault along with the sword. His men had all been sent back home to their own time with no memory of what had transpired. Could it be one of them? Could her spell somehow have failed? That would be unlikely, but she could not shake the feeling that was exactly what had happened.

Once Maggie and Dylan were in place in Edinburgh she hoped they'd have the answers to her questions. Patience would be needed, but in the meantime she was determined to find out what she could from her place by the hearth. First she would contact Anania.

Edna stared into the flames and called to Anania. She didn't have to wait long for a reply.

"Edna, I'm here," Anania said.

"I wanted ye to ken what is happening. Maggie and Dylan will be leaving for Edinburgh today. They'll do their best to convince the Sinclairs to allow ye to take their daughter back to Aleck Sinclair. 'Twill nae be easy, but I have faith that they can do it."

"I'll be waiting to hear from ye. I'll be ready to take the bairn with me. I'll be sure she is well taken care of until we can get her to Laird Sinclair."

"Good. Anania, do ye ken who this man is?"

"Nay. All I know is that Ariweth has summoned him, much the way he summoned the other man."

"I wish I knew who it was. I'm questioning a spell that I wove around Malcolm Granger's men. I'm nae sure it held."

"Ariweth is a powerful sorcerer, even from his prison. If there was a way I could destroy him forever, I would. For now, all I can do is keep him imprisoned and try to keep him from finding a way to free himself."

"I'm here to help ye, Anania. Anything at all I can do, I will."

"I ken it, Edna. Yer a good friend to us and we are here for ye if yer ever in need."

"We'll speak again soon." Edna waved a hand at the fire and Anania was gone.

Edna felt a warmth and kinship with the elves and faeries. She'd had a special relationship with them for as long as she could remember. It was common practice for them to help each other and she hoped that together they could save the young bairn. Failure on their part would be devastating to all of them. She vowed to find a way to rid the world of Ariweth. It was the least she felt she could do.

"Maggie, I love Edna as if she were my own mother, but I'm not so sure this is a job you and I can handle." Dylan pulled their suitcases out of the closet and set them on the bed.

"She wouldn't ask us to do it if she didn't believe we could," she replied, adding clothes to her empty suitcase. "When it comes to magic, the police can't help. First of all, they wouldn't believe the magic part of the story and secondly, ye cannae fight magic the way ye would any other criminal activity.

"I can't fight magic at all," Dylan said.

"But I can. And between me, Aunt Edna and Anania, we will keep the babe safe." To Maggie, this seemed like a fairly easy assignment. Befriend a young couple and help to keep their child from harm. Although most people scoff at the idea of witches and magic, she knew she could convince them to trust her. "I love your confidence," Dylan said.

"Thank ye, husband," Maggie eyed the movement of his muscles as he packed. They would have a lot of time alone in Edinburgh, Maggie realized. There would be no need for Dylan to be up before dawn to make breakfast for the guests. They could sleep late and make this a nice little vacation. She pictured the two of them cuddled up in bed, her hands...

"There. I'm done," he said, closing the suitcase and throwing his hands in the air. "I win."

Maggie was pulled from her daydream to see Dylan grinning at her. "I didnae ken this was a competition. If I had known I would be the winner."

Dylan caught the look in her eye and stalked towards her, his voice low and sexy, "I had to ensure my victory. You have an unfair advantage. You're a witch," he teased.

"Why didnae I think of that?"

"Finish your packing and I'll show you what I've won," he said, winking.

"We've nae time for that, love," Maggie said, shaking her head at him.

He appeared greatly disappointed. How could she resist those puppy dog eyes? The answer was she had to. "Don't look so sad. Check back in with me when we get to the hotel in Edinburgh," she said, and turned from him to pull a few things from the closet.

"Speaking of hotels, where are we staying?"

"I'm nae sure, but Auntie will have a place in mind. She's probably already made the reservations for us."

"I hope it's nice," was his reply.

"I hope so, too." Maggie knew Edna would place them exactly

where they needed to be in Edinburgh, but she had no idea what that meant for their accommodations. She closed and zipped her suitcase. "Done."

"I'll go get the car. You meet me out front," Dylan took both of their suitcases to bring downstairs.

"Wait," Maggie said.

He stopped in his tracks and glanced back at her.

"I love you, Dylan." She walked up to him and placed a passion-filled kiss on his lips. He dropped both suitcases and wrapped his arms around her, holding her close. She could feel the hardness of his body pressed against her and wished they weren't in such a hurry.

Pulling back, Dylan gazed into her deep green eyes. "I love you, too, but as you reminded me, we don't have time." He chuckled as he retrieved the suitcases. "You've given me something to look forward to once we get to the hotel."

Maggie laughed, thinking how lucky she was to have found Dylan. With him by her side she could accomplish anything, even a task of such monumental importance, like this one.

CHAPTER 3

A RRIVING IN EDINBURGH, Dylan checked his phone for the location of their hotel. When she'd made the reservation, Edna made sure that it would be in close proximity to the couple they needed to contact. It couldn't have turned out better, they were practically across the street from Maureen and David Sinclair and their little daughter, Molly.

"What now?" Dylan asked.

"I think it would be best to meet them in the most natural way possible," Maggie replied.

"And what would that be?"

"There's a bakery across the street. Auntie told me that Maureen works there, so we should go sit and have coffee there." Maggie opened her suitcase and started removing her clothes and placing them on hangers in the closet.

"Okay. Won't she think it's weird if I just introduce myself as her cousin?" Dylan asked.

Maggie rolled her eyes. "That's not how we'll do it. Let me handle it. Just follow my lead."

She finished unpacking her bag and then opened Dylan's.

"You can just leave my stuff," he said.

"Dylan, we dinnae ken how long we're going to be here. It'll be much easier if we put your things away."

"Okay. You're the boss." He gave her one of his patently Dylan smiles, which always made her tummy do flip flops and her heart beat a little faster. "By the way, I haven't forgotten what you said

13

back at the inn."

"Neither have I," she said. "It'll have to wait until we come back."

They finished unpacking before heading downstairs and across the street.

THE MAYFLOUR BAKERY and Sweet Shop was in a quaint older neighborhood. Its name was scrolled across the glass windows that faced the street in big, bold letters. On entering, the first thing Maggie and Dylan noticed was a large glass case filled with cookies, muffins, scones and cakes, which divided the room between the eating area filled with tables in the front and the kitchen itself in the back. Black and white honeycomb tiles set in a vintage pattern adorned the floor and the walls were covered with photographs of customers posing with the owners or eating a delicious treat. It had a comfortable, homey and warm feel about it.

"Good day to ye," a woman behind the counter said.

Dylan noted she would be too old to be Maureen. "Good day. It smells amazing in here."

"Thank ye. I've just taken some scones from the oven." The woman smiled proudly as she began to place them on a tray to cool.

"Should we give them a try?" Dylan asked Maggie.

"Aye. They do look good," Maggie said, looking over the goodies in the case.

"Have a seat anywhere ye like and I'll bring them to ye. Would ye care for some tea as well?"

"Yes, please," Dylan answered.

Maggie was still examining all the other baked goods. "Everything looks so good!"

The woman smiled and leaned toward Maggie with a conspiratorial wink, "I'll bring ye a selection. How does that sound?"

"Delicious," Maggie said, smiling warmly at the woman. She

and Dylan took a seat by the window overlooking the street.

A side door opened and a young woman came in. "I'm sorry I'm late, Mrs. May. I had to wait for David to come back to look after Molly."

"That's her," Dylan whispered to Maggie.

"You're a regular Sherlock Holmes," she teased.

Maureen put on an apron and moved behind the counter.

"Here, dear, would ye be so kind as to bring the lovely folks over there these goodies, while I get their tea ready." Mrs. May handed a tray to Maureen.

She took the tray and smiled brightly as she walked towards Maggie and Dylan. "Good morning," she said.

"Good morning," Maggie replied.

The scones, along with a muffin, a croissant and some shortbread cookies were placed in front of them along with clotted cream and jam. "Yer tea will be along shortly."

"Thank you. Could I ask you a question?" Maggie said.

"Aye." Maureen brushed her hands down the front of her apron. "What can I help ye with?"

"We're visiting from out of town and we're trying to decide what we should do while we're here. Any suggestions?"

Dylan was letting Maggie do all the talking. She was very good at putting people at ease.

"Of course," Maureen's eyes sparkled. She clearly enjoyed talking about her city. "Ye'll definitely want to visit the castle. It sits atop Castle Rock, which is an extinct volcano. There's been a castle there since about the twelfth century." She put her finger to her lips, thinking. "You might also enjoy Holyrood Palace, it's the Queen's official residence when she's in Scotland. Oh, and the Royal Botanic Gardens are a must see. So many beautiful plants and flowers, especially the rhododendrons. And Arthur's Seat, which sits atop another extinct volcano. Do ye enjoy whisky?"

"Yes. Very much," Dylan responded.

"There are some distillery tours ye can go on. I think ye'd enjoy them. I believe there are some brochures in the rack by the counter."

"Sounds great. Thank ye," Maggie said.

"Where are ye here from?" Maureen asked.

"We're visiting from Glendaloch. My Aunt Edna owns The Thistle & Hive Inn there." Maggie picked up her tea cup and took a sip.

"Oh, lovely."

"And my husband," Maggie nodded at Dylan, "is the chef and baker for the inn."

"Aye. So ye ken a good scone when ye've eaten one," Maureen chuckled. "What do ye think of ours?"

Dylan had just taken a big bite, so was unable to speak.

"I'll give ye a moment to savor them and be right back with yer tea." Maureen walked back into the kitchen where they could hear her putting together the tea tray.

"Now all we have to do is introduce ourselves. When she hears our last name we'll be golden," Maggie said.

Dylan swallowed the last bit of scone in his mouth just as Maureen returned with their tea and some brochures.

"Well, what do ye think?" she asked.

"Amazing. Better than mine," he replied.

"Mrs. May, he says yer scones are better than his," Maureen turned to tell the older woman. She was balancing another large tray of scones with one hand and clearing a spot for it with the other.

"Well, thank ye, son," she called from behind the counter.

"You're welcome. What's your secret?"

"'Tis an old family recipe and I'm sworn to secrecy, but I can tell ye that 'tis best to let the dough rest a while before ye work it."

"Thanks. I'll keep that in mind," he said.

"Would ye care for another?" Maureen asked.

"I think we'll take some for later, and bag up the rest of the things we haven't eaten."

"They do make a nice treat."

Dylan held out his hand to Mrs. May. "I'm Dylan Sinclair and

16

this is my wife, Maggie. It's been a pleasure to meet you. I'm sure we'll be back. We're staying right across the street."

Maureen stopped as she wiped one of the tables and straightened. "I'm a Sinclair as well."

"Are ye really?" Maggie asked, attempting to put just the right amount of surprise in her voice.

"Aye. I wonder if we're related," Maureen said.

"Could be. I've been doing a lot of family history research lately. I'll take a look and see if there's a Maureen Sinclair in my tree," Dylan said.

"It would be my husband ye'd be searching for. His name's David," Maureen offered.

"Wouldn't it be funny if we were cousins or something?" Dylan said, a wide smile lighting his face.

Maureen was examining his face. "Ye ken, ye do look a bit like my David."

"Do I?" Dylan brushed a wayward blond curl out of his eyes. "I'll have to meet him."

"He's watching our daughter Molly right now. She's napping. If you can come back a bit later, I'll see to it that he's here."

"Great. In the meantime, I've got my laptop with me. I'll take a look at that family tree."

Mrs. May was chuckling to herself. "'Tis a truly small world. To think that of all the bake shops in Edinburgh ye could've wandered into for a scone and some tea, you chose mine. I can hardly wait to find out if ye've found yer long lost relative."

"I wouldn't say he was lost, but simply not known to me," Dylan said. "Maggie, we should go." He turned to Mrs. May and Maureen. "We'll be back later."

They paid their bill and collected the box of scones and treats from Mrs. May before heading back across the street to their room.

CHAPTER 4

Pierce Holmes watched the couple leaving the bakery from his hotel room window. He'd chosen his room wisely. From here he was able to keep a close watch on the Sinclairs and whenever they left their apartment, he was quickly downstairs and out following them where ever they decided to go. So far he hadn't had any luck in finding the best time to strike, but he had to make his move soon. There were times when he wondered just what he was doing here and almost headed to the airport to go back home to San Francisco, but then something would come over him and he'd be even more determined than ever to succeed with his plans.

Up until a few weeks ago, Pierce had been happy believing that his boss, Malcolm Granger had gone off on some crazy adventure and that he was merely looking after things until he returned. The fact that he hadn't heard from him in months wasn't necessarily concerning. Malcolm had always been very secretive about his travels and so Pierce, believing he was off somewhere searching for ancient artifacts, had been living in Malcolm's modern day medieval castle and working out of his top floor office since he'd been gone. Malcolm wouldn't like the fact that he'd been taking advantage of the situation in order to enjoy the luxuries afforded him at the castle, but he'd never know. The place was so big a person could get lost in it and he was pretty sure Malcolm didn't use half of it anyway. Pierce simply made sure to stay away from Malcolm's suite of rooms and that left him plenty of room to roam.

It had been Pierce's daily routine to head to the massive skyscraper that housed Malcolm Granger's office and business headquarters. Sitting high atop the skyline of the city, Pierce could see all the way across the bay to Oakland. As he gazed out the window, he would try without success to fill the gaps in his memory. For some reason he couldn't recall anything that happened after the competition at the Ren Faire. That was the last time he remembered seeing Malcolm. Despite this lapse in memory, he felt it was his duty to continue doing his job, which meant that when Malcolm was away, Pierce was in charge. He'd been through the papers on his boss's desk numerous times and thought he'd taken care of everything, when he came across an ancient document he was sure hadn't been there the day before. That moment would change everything, setting him on the path to Edinburgh. As he read, the legend about the Sinclair daughter enticed him to the point of becoming an obsession. He had to get his hands on Molly Sinclair. She was the key to the vault that held the Twin Sword. He wanted all the power and wealth the sword would give him. A sense of self-importance took hold of him. He'd never been a leader, but he felt an unexpected strength and surety coursing through his veins. He had to have that sword and he was willing to do whatever was necessary to get it.

Pierce had a natural aptitude for running Malcolm's empire. After all, he had been his right-hand man before the unthinkable happened. It's strange how he didn't remember anything about where Malcom had gone or when he might return until he came across that ancient document about the Sinclairs. The very moment he held it in his hands he relived everything that had happened on their time travel journey to medieval Scotland. He broke out in a cold sweat recalling the details of their doomed expedition. They'd been searching for the Twin Sword and had just found its resting place when they were attacked on all sides by Highlanders. An instant hatred of Edna Campbell took root in his head. The terror he'd felt upon seeing her charging towards them with her horde of warriors almost knocked him off his feet. She was the reason that Malcolm was dead. She was the one who stood in the way of him retrieving the sword. One thing he knew for certain, as soon as he got his hands on the Twin Sword, he meant to exact revenge for his boss. She would be its first victim. The Twin Sword became the most important thing in the world to him, just as it had been for Malcolm, and nothing would stop him from getting his hands on it. Consumed with hatred, he had a barely controllable urge to go across the street and snatch the Sinclair child right then and there, but he had to temper his wants with what made sense and that was to continue waiting for his moment. It would come. He knew it would. He only wished it would happen soon.

"That went well," Dylan noted as they passed through the lobby on their way to the elevator.

"I told you it would." Maggie pushed the button for the elevator and then leaned into Dylan. He put an arm around her and kissed the top of her head.

The doors to the elevator opened and a man walked out. Maggie's senses were suddenly on high alert as she turned and watched him walk through the front doors and out onto the street.

"What's wrong?" Dylan asked, following her gaze.

"That man. I think he's the one." She sniffed the air and nodded her head. An icy chill had followed him as he passed.

"I thought I was the one," Dylan said with a hint of mischief in his voice.

He was rewarded with a scowl from Maggie that sobered him immediately. "Is he the guy who's after Molly Sinclair?" Dylan looked as if he might run after him and Maggie laid a hand on his arm to stop him.

"Aye. I can't explain it, but… I could feel it. Feel his evil intent."

"Should we go after him?" Dylan asked, body tensing and ready to run.

"Nay. He willnae make his move now," Maggie replied.

"How do you know that?"

"I just do." Maggie wasn't sure how to explain the feeling. "Call it intuition or my abilities as a witch, but I dinnae believe he *can* do anything right now." She shivered and quickly entered the elevator with Dylan right behind her.

"Maggie, this worries me. Does he have abilities?" Dylan peered out of the elevator.

"Nay. He doesnae, but the one who controls him does." She did her best to keep the worry from her voice, willing him to relax.

"So for me, a fight with him is a fair fight," he stated.

"Aye. 'Tis his master that we must be concerned with." The doors closed and they felt the elevator start to climb. The last thing she wanted to do was to have him worrying before there was a need to. She attempted to relax and smiled at her husband. "I'm feeling a bit worn. I'd like to rest a bit if ye dinnae mind." She wrapped her arms around Dylan's waist, feeling his abs tighten as she did. She could feel his easy-going nature return as he nuzzled her hair with his nose as the doors to the elevator opened on their floor.

"Of course not. I'll join you."

"We've got some time before we have to be back across the street." She exited the elevator and began the short walk to their door swaying her hips to and fro in an enticing manner she knew would pique Dylan's interest. He was right behind her, giving her a loving pat on the bottom as she opened the door to their room.

Pierce Holmes noted the couple waiting for the elevator as he walked past them. They were the same couple he'd seen exiting the bakery. The woman had seemed particularly interested in him. She'd sniffed the air as he passed. He wondered if she was the one who had been watching him. The one he couldn't see. If she was, he knew he had to make his move soon. The paranoia he was feeling was getting worse. Prior to finding the papers, he'd been anything but paranoid. Now his mind was filled with thoughts that made him completely uncomfortable in his own skin. He couldn't stop them. Even sleeping wasn't a relief as his dreams were filled with unseen threats that surrounded him and filled him with fear.

He stood on the sidewalk outside of the hotel and tried to shake off this intense veil of darkness that was surrounding him. It did no good, it never did. As he'd learned in the past few weeks, it was better to accept it and follow his instincts no matter how strange it seemed.

He crossed the street and stared in the window of The Mayflour Bakery before deciding to enter. He was greeted by the elderly lady who owned the bakery.

"Mrs. May," he said, nodding his head in her direction before sitting with his back to the wall giving him a view of the entire bakery.

"Mr. Holmes. Good to see ye again," she said. "Yer usual?"

"Yes, please." Someone left a copy of The Edinburgh Evening News, which he picked up and perused. It was good cover for him when Maureen Sinclair emerged from the kitchen and began sweeping the floors around him.

"Here ye go." Mrs. May placed a cup of tea in front of him along with a plate of crumpets.

"Thank you," he said, maintaining his position behind the news-paper.

He heard the side door open and peeked his head around to see who was entering the bakery.

"There's my wee lass," Maureen said, taking Molly from her father's arms.

"She just woke up," David said. "Got a good long nap, she did."

This was perfect, better than Pierce could have hoped for. Mother, father and child all here in the bakery alone with him and Mrs. May. He folded up the newspaper and placed it on the table in preparation. Ready to make his move, he placed his hand into his jacket where he'd carefully concealed a dirk. He wrapped his fingers around it and was just about to stand when the bell above the door began to ring and several teenaged boys and girls entered the bakery laughing and talking. The girls were interested in wee Molly, while the boys were interested in the girls and the baked goods. He cursed under his breath. He could wait for them to leave or he could come back later. What would it be? While he thought about it, David left the bakery with the child by way of the side door. His decision was made for him. So far kidnapping Molly was turning out to be a lot harder than he'd anticipated. He stood and sipped the last of his tea, wrapped the uneaten crumpets in a napkin and slid them into his pocket. He'd be back later.

CHAPTER 5

Isla Mackall wasn't happy. Accompanying her brother Nick and his wife Kat to visit Aleck Sinclair was far from what she wished. She had a sneaking suspicion that they were planning a match between the laird and either her sister, Merry, or herself. Merry, who rode along beside her, would be the far better choice to become Lady Sinclair. She was sweet, kind and so much better at managing a household than Isla could ever be. There was no doubt in her mind that given the choice, Aleck Sinclair would choose her sister and therefore, she could see no reason at all to be on this journey.

"Isla, ye look as if ye've something bitter in yer mouth," Nick observed.

"Aye. 'Tis this trek ye've forced me on." She eyed him with a bit of sisterly venom.

"Do ye nae wish to spend time with us?" he asked, feigning hurt feelings.

Isla lifted an eyebrow in his direction. She wouldn't dignify him with an answer. Instead she harrumphed loudly and soured her expression even further.

Kat and Merry chuckled at the exchange taking place between Nick and Isla.

"Isla, I wouldnae wish to make this journey without ye," Merry said, becoming serious.

"'Tis sweet of ye, but ye ken ye'd be fine without me," Isla answered.

Merry appeared thoughtful at her sister's words. "Yer right. I would be, but I love spending time with ye and I'd miss ye as well."

Isla smiled at her sweet wee sister. How could she deny her wish? "And I love spending time with ye." She'd deal with her frustration and do her best not to let it show.

"I cannae wait to see Aleck," Kat said. "I can hardly believe I've a brother."

"Ye must spend some time with him. Get to know him," Nick offered.

"Aye. I will. But, I'm looking forward to our trip to Edinburgh as well."

Isla had a sneaking suspicion that some unspoken message was being exchanged between Nick and Kat. They were up to something, of that she was sure.

A heavy mist followed them on their journey across emerald green fields and rocky tors. Merry had chatted excitedly despite the weather and Isla's bad mood. Nothing seemed to dampen her spirits. As luck would have it, and as Merry had continuously said it would, the sun finally broke through the clouds, banishing the mist and making the remainder of their journey much more tolerable.

Approaching a stream, Kat turned to Nick. "I'd like to bathe before we reach Sinclair Castle."

"Aye. I agree," Nick said. "After two days on horseback, I think we'll all look and feel much better once we do."

Isla grimaced at this.

"Yer making that sour face again," Nick said, gazing at Isla. "Do ye nae wish to bathe?"

She glared at him. "Nae. The water will be cold."

"Ye look a sight. 'Twould be best if ye did."

They were quickly approaching a swiftly flowing river. Isla's heart began to race in her chest. She couldn't swim. Didn't Nick know this?

They rode downstream until they came to a pool of water that would be safer for their purposes. Everyone dismounted except Isla who remained astride her horse, unwilling to subject herself to the terror she knew would come if she was forced into the water. Nick and his men removed themselves to an area of the river that was not far from them, but which would allow the women their privacy.

"If ye need me, shout," Nick said as he walked away.

Kat and Merry began to remove their clothes, laying them out on some nearby rocks before diving into the cool water of the pool.

"Oh, 'tis cold," Kat said as she broke the surface of the water.

"Isla, join us," Merry called.

"Ye ken I dinnae like the water," Isla replied. She dismounted and sat on a rock to watch the two women as they cavorted in the pool.

"Ye'll nae make a good impression on Laird Sinclair," Merry tried.

"I dinnae care what Laird Sinclair thinks of me," Isla barked. She didn't wish to be paraded before Aleck Sinclair as if she were a prized cow. "'Tis nae me that he's wanting to see, Merry."

Merry stopped what she was doing and glanced her way with an arched brow. "I thought ye liked the laird. He's quite handsome."

"Just because he's handsome doesnae mean that I like him."

"But at the wedding…"The expression on Isla's face made Merry rethink her words. "Come in. 'Tis nae cold any longer."

"Merry, yer lips disagree with what yer saying. They're turning blue. Ye should come out of the water and get dressed." Isla stood and walked to their bags. The sooner they were out of the water and dressed, the sooner she could relax.

Merry turned to Kat, who took a good look and nodded agreement. "Come. Let's get out and dry off."

Isla met them both with towels and helped them get dry. She didn't wish to think about Kat and Nick's wedding. That was the first time she'd met Aleck Sinclair and there had been an instant connection between the two of them. It wasn't just his handsome face she'd been attracted to. It was the confident masculinity he exuded that had drawn her in. He'd shown his true colors though. After flirting with her he'd gone after Merry. She'd found them in the barn together. Granted they weren't doing anything to be

26

ashamed of, but if she hadn't arrived when she did who knows what might have happened.

The women dressed and then they were joined by Nick. Everyone appeared refreshed, except Isla who knew she must look awful, but she'd be damned if she were going to make herself pretty for any man.

Merry and Kat fixed each other's hair and then turned to Isla who merely shook her head at them.

"Just let us fix yer hair," Kat said. "'Tis all knotted. Ye'll have a hard time combing it yerself."

Isla relented. The only thing she hated more than fussing over her appearance was running a comb through her tangled locks. "Just a simple braid," she warned Kat.

"Aye. A simple braid," Kat replied.

Isla sat back and found herself relaxing as Kat carefully worked the comb through her hair. As much as she hated to admit it, she was enjoying the attention her sister-in-law was giving her. She wasn't used to having things done for her. The Mackall household was a busy, bustling place and she had no interest in pampering. Isla preferred to spend her time with the men on the practice field. Something that no one in her family seemed to understand. It was where she felt the most comfortable. She wanted to be a warrior. To go into battle with the men of the castle, not be relegated to stitch work or other womanly endeavors.

When Kat was done, she stood back to look at Isla. "Aleck will think ye a great beauty."

Grumpiness returned. "I dinnae care what Aleck thinks." She watched as Kat chuckled and then walked away. "And I'm nae a great beauty!" she called after her.

Why did they not listen to her? This was going to be a humiliating experience for her and none of them seemed to care. Perhaps they needed to see with their own eyes that Aleck would choose Merry and not her. Then they would leave her be and let her go back to the life she wanted.

Merry presented her with an apple. "Ye should eat something. Nick says it will be a few more hours before we reach our destination."

Isla took the apple. "Thank ye, Merry." She took a bite, enjoying the tart, crispness of it.

Merry sat down next to her. "Isla, why do ye nae wish to see Aleck?"

Isla didn't answer. She had a mouthful of apple and it seemed a good excuse to be silent.

"Ye ken when ye found us in the barn. Aleck didnae have any designs on me. He came along as a friend."

"Is that what ye think?" Isla wasn't quite so sure she agreed with her sister.

"'Tis ye he likes," Merry assured her.

Isla stared at the ground. She knew her sister was trying to be kind. "He'd be better off liking ye, Merry. I'm nae interested in being anyone's wife."

"But why?" Merry asked.

"Ye ken why. I'll nae say another word about it." Isla stood and marched off knowing Merry knew better than to follow.

ON THEIR WAY again, Isla kept silent. Her mind wandered back to her home, Dunnet Head, and the men who'd taught her all about battle. Over the last few years she'd learned so much from them. Training with them had given her purpose when everything else seemed so dark. It was the place where she was free to be herself and free of the past. Now, she could use a sword as well as any man, and was equally as good with a bow. If it came down to it, none of the men she trained with doubted her ability to do whatever it took to be victorious in battle. They understood her and they never treated her as if she were some fragile flower that would wither and die if exposed to the sun and wind. They respected her. She treasured this above all else.

Her family knew this and they understood it, to some extent, but that didn't stop them from encouraging her to be more of a woman. What they didn't understand was that she'd stopped being a woman the day her Derrick died. She'd cried her last tear and sealed her heart away from any chance she would feel anything that could hurl her down a bottomless pit of pain ever again. She could not describe herself as happy. Not like Merry and her continuous optimism. And not even like Kat, who was more serious but always kind and sweet to everyone in the castle. But happiness was a small price to pay. If she could keep herself from feeling, it was all for the best.

"Isla, I'm concerned about ye," Nick said as he rode up beside her.

"Whatever for. I'm fine."

"So you say, but I dinnae believe ye." His brotherly concern was evident.

"I'm sorry. I dinnae mean to be difficult. I promise I'll try to be more pleasant."

"'Tis not what I mean at all and ye ken it." Nick turned his horse around to her side and they stopped. "Ye cannae spend the rest of yer life this way. Ye must let others into yer world."

Isla clenched her teeth. She knew what she had to do and everyone needed to stop bothering her about it. "I can spend my life how I see fit, brother. I have everyone I need in my world, thank you." She was regretting that she'd just told Nick she'd do her best to be pleasant.

Nick did not even blink. Instead he reached for her hand and gave it a small squeeze. "Yer missing out on so much. We all love ye and care about ye. We want ye to be happy."

Her heart softened a bit. Nick had been gone for two years and was only recently restored to the family. She had missed him so much during that time and was thankful he was back with their mother and the clan at Dunnet Head. They did love her, although she certainly didn't know why. She wasn't easy to be around and she knew it. It was her only defense against the thing she feared the most, dreaded the most. She couldn't bear the thought of losing any of them. She bit back the tears that threatened. She wouldn't cry. She never did.

"Isla, please. Open yer heart once again. Allow yerself to be loved. Me heart breaks fer what ye've been through. For what yer going through now."

She didn't let him finish his thought. "I'm fine. I've told ye." He didn't understand what she had been through. None of them did. "Now, please leave me be. I promised I would be pleasant and I will keep me word."

Nick rode along beside her in silence. The grim look on his face was unusual for him, but she wouldn't alleviate it with lies about love and happiness. She simply wouldn't.

NICK DROPPED BACK to ride with Kat, leaving his sister Merry to deal with Isla.

"She'll be fine," Kat assured him.

"I'm nae so sure." Nick watched Merry ride close to Isla and start chattering away. He couldn't hear what she was saying but her bright smile and easy laughter floated back to them as they rode. It was his responsibility to see his sisters settled. He had missed out on a lot while he was gone, but was determined to make up for that absence by being the big brother they needed.

"'Tis her life and her choice, ye ken." Kat's voice drew his attention from his sisters. "If she doesnae wish to marry, then we should leave her be."

"I want her to ken the happiness I've found with ye," he said, glancing over at his beautiful wife.

"I want that for her as well, but if she doesnae wish it we cannae force it." Nick could see Merry work her magic. The tension had drained from Isla's shoulders and he could almost make out a hint of a smile when she looked back at him over her shoulder. She knew something was up, that there was more to this trip than taking Kat to visit her brother. Aleck Sinclair had proven himself a great friend, and for some reason he was interested in pursuing Isla. The match made sense as far as forming an alliance, but he would never push his sisters to marry for his own gain. He stole another look at his beautiful wife. There was a time when he had thought he would have to give her up and marry another out of duty. His heart ached at the very thought of missing a moment of happiness with Kat. No. He would not force or cajole his sister into marrying anyone. Besides, watching Aleck attempt to soften his sister's heart might prove entertaining.

"Yer brother will have one hell of a time winning her over."

"Something tells me he's quite capable when it comes to women," Kat laughed.

"Yer right. I'm nae a lass and even I can see it," he joked.

Kat reached out to hold his hand, which he gladly surrendered to her. "We are lucky, ye ken?"

"The luckiest," he agreed.

"We're good examples of what love is. 'Tis good for both yer sisters to see it."

"They see it and they ken it, but Isla…" Nick thought back to the days when Isla had been a very opinionated little lass. He could see her now, standing hands on hips berating one of the young stable lads because he'd not given her horse enough feed. She'd been a feisty wee one, full of life, her big brown eyes lit from within with a zest for life. He wished more than anything he could take away her pain and once again see her that spark in her… that passion.

"She's been broken-hearted for too long. I fear she cannae get away from it," Kat said.

He knew Kat was right. Isla had retreated into a hard shell that couldn't be cracked. She was protecting herself from feeling. From loving anyone ever again. Maybe this was too soon. Maybe they should have waited for this, but Aleck was ready to be married now and Isla was the one he wanted. And so they made this journey to give him the opportunity to woo her and if that failed, there was always Merry.

As they neared their destination, Nick was grateful for the warm sun on his face. The slow steady pace of their horses reflected the leisurely attitude of the group. Nick and his men weren't off to battle. This was an enjoyable trek. An occasional nesting bird was disturbed by their passing, but no other creatures seemed to be about this day. The long grass swayed in the soft breeze that ruffled Nick's hair and he felt a certain peace traveling with his wife, and his sisters. As much as he loved the sounds of the ocean at Dunnet Head, he was enjoying the quiet here. The only sounds were those of the horses' hooves softly plodding along the dirt path that would lead them to Sinclair Castle.

Differences in the landscape were evident all around them. Unlike home, where the vastness of the sea was visible from every vantage point, Sinclair Castle stood more inland. It was set upon a hill top with a complete view of the surrounding lands. Once an ancient hill fort, it was now home to a grand, expansive castle. If an enemy were to approach, they would be seen from any direction and at quite a distance and for this reason, Nick had no doubt that Aleck Sinclair was already aware of their approach. They were gradually leaving flat lands and heading up towards the top of the hill. They rode single file now as the path they followed had begun to narrow as they climbed. The ground was strewn with rocks and bordered by green plants and shrubs and so Nick rode first, setting their trail and was followed close behind by Kat, Merry and Isla. His men were right behind them.

CHAPTER 6

S ITTING ATOP HIS destrier Brychan, Aleck Sinclair rode out to welcome his guests. He'd been informed by his scouts that they would be arriving this morning and wanted to be the first to greet them. The sun was shining for the first time in days warming the air enough that he had no need of his cloak. He rode to the top of a rocky outcropping which overlooked the valley below and was pleased to see Nick Mackall and his family making their way up a path worn into the craggy hillside by so many others who'd passed this way before.

He raised his arm to wave as Nick gazed up at him. He could clearly make out Kat, riding behind him and then the two sisters, Merry and Isla. He knew immediately which was Isla despite the fact that both women wore their hoods to protect them from the sunny but cool weather. Isla sat up straight and tall in the saddle, while Merry's daintiness was obvious in the softness of the way she held the reigns. Aleck grinned broadly. He was looking forward to courting Isla. She'd shown him she would be a challenge, which is just what he wanted in a woman. Merry was lovely and sweet, but somehow he knew that Isla's sharp tongue would keep him on his toes. She would keep life exciting and he could possibly spend all his days exploring the many sides to her that he'd come to know in their short meeting at Kat and Nick's wedding.

He watched her expertly maneuver the craggy hill, reaching down occasionally to encourage her horse with words or pats on the neck. She paused in her climb to look out over the land that had been his home and his responsibility all of his life. He knew every rock, every stream, every secret hiding place. He suddenly wanted to know what she was thinking about as she took in the beautiful landscape. Was she pleased?

At that moment, her head turned towards him and he watched her eyes slowly take in his horse, then him. When she realized he was watching her, she suddenly pulled her hood farther over her face and turned away. He couldn't help but smile.

ISLA'S EYES BRIEFLY met Aleck's before she quickly hid them from his view. In that moment, she had been struck once again by how handsome he was. Sitting proudly atop his horse, he was the picture of the perfect Highland warrior. She couldn't imagine there were many who would want to tangle with him. Broad shoulders and well-muscled arms and chest were hard not to notice. A feeling she'd missed for quite some time fluttered in her belly. She reminded herself that this man was meant for her sister, not for her.

"Do ye see him?" Merry asked, turning in the saddle to look at Isla.

"Aye. I see him," Isla replied.

"Are ye nae excited to finally be here?" The sweet look of concern on Merry's face was too much for Isla.

"Ye ken I dinnae wish to be here," she snapped.

Merry turned back away from her. Isla felt terrible. Merry only wanted her to be happy and no matter how hard she tried, she just couldn't bring herself to share in her sister's excitement.

Nick picked up the pace and everyone behind him followed suit, his men bringing up the rear as they had throughout the trip. She should have ridden behind with them, but it wouldn't have been right. She was a Mackall, but Isla felt more at home with them than she did with her brother and sister. There was no reason for it. They'd always been kind to her and loved her even when she'd

34

been most unlovable.

"Aleck!" Nick called. "'Tis good to see ye." Nick rode to Aleck's side and the two men grasped each other's arms in greeting.

"How was your journey?" Aleck asked, surveying the others.

"Aside from the weather, it was without incident," Nick reported.

"Kat. How is my beautiful sister?" Aleck asked as he rode to his sister's side. He leaned across to kiss her cheek.

"Happy to be here," she beamed.

"Well, I'm happy to have ye." He squeezed her hands before moving on to the sisters. "Good day to ye, Merry!"

"Good day, Aleck." Merry blushed, suddenly becoming quite shy.

"Isla. 'Tis good to see ye again. I hope ye'll enjoy yer stay here." Not receiving an answer, he turned his horse towards the castle. "Shall we?" He rode alongside Nick and Kat, making conversation the whole way back to his home. Aleck signaled to the man atop the barbican, letting him know that all was well. They rode into the courtyard and Aleck immediately dismounted, going to the women to help them down from their mounts. Merry was grateful for the help, as was Kat. When he reached Isla, she had already dismounted and purposely glanced away from him.

A knowing smile crossed his lips as he turned back to Nick. "There is room for your men in the soldier's quarters."

"Alan, see to the horses," Nick said.

"Aye, sir."

The Mackall family followed Aleck through the castle doors and into the great hall, where servants were at hand to take their cloaks and provide them with food and drink.

"Shall we have a bite to eat before I show you to your rooms?"

ALECK SHOWED THEM to seats at the high table. He held out a chair for Merry, but once again when he turned to Isla she had already seated herself. "I'm going to have to be faster where yer concerned," he chuckled and much to Isla's chagrin, sat down next to her.

The close proximity of his body to hers caused heat to course through her highly sensitized core. She fanned herself with her hand to cool down, but with little luck. Butterflies churned in her belly as her breathing came in short, shallow gasps. Her own body was betraying her and it wasn't sitting well with her. She should be able to control these things, but for the life of her she couldn't do it.

Aleck rose and stood behind her chair. "Ye seem to be overheating. Let me help ye remove yer cloak." His hands brushed her shoulders as he grasped the edges of her cloak.

"Nae. I'll see to it." She shooed his hands away and slid the cloak from her shoulders.

"Yer quite the independent lass, arenae ye?" Aleck asked as he sat beside her again.

She wasn't sure that needed an answer and so she didn't. She quickly glanced his way only to find his bold green eyes and dimpled cheeks smiling at her. Why on earth was he looking at her like that? She was feeling quite flustered as she took in his mesmerizing eyes and handsome face so she quickly looked away. Her hands seemed to want to reach out and touch him, but Isla firmly grasped the fabric of her dress to keep them from doing so. "How was yer journey?" he asked, the velvety baritone of his voice sent shivers through her already over stimulated body.

"Unnecessary," she stated. She was being rude and she knew it. She'd promised Nick she'd try hard to be pleasant, but considering that this visit was already too long, she had a feeling that these next few weeks were going to be the longest of her life. She couldn't remember a time when she'd felt so uncomfortable. Aleck Sinclair was purposely doing his best to get under her skin and it was working. She only hoped it wasn't as obvious to him as it was to her.

Aleck for his part, seemed pleased with her despite her curt answers. He chuckled and she looked away feeling a strange tenseness taking over her body. She wished to bolt from the room, believing fresh air would help alleviate these strange sensations she was having towards her host.

The servants brought bowls of warm water for them to wash their hands and towels to dry them. Pitchers of wine, ale and water were all placed on the table within easy reach.

"Isla, may I pour you some wine?" Aleck asked before she could reach for it herself.

"Thank ye," she replied.

He poured wine for himself as well and then raised his cup in a toast. "To my good friend, Nick. Thanks to ye and yer family for making a home for my sister. And to ye, Kat. I didnae believe the day would ever come when ye and I would share a meal together. Now that we've been reunited, I pray that we'll have many more visits like this."

All eyes turned to Kat, who was beaming at her brother. Isla was happy for her. She'd come to care deeply for Kat and enjoyed having her as a sister.

They all gladly raised their cups to her, saying, "Slainte."

Aleck's eyes wandered to Isla's face. Her soulful brown eyes were large and expressive. He could get lost in them. Her hair was neatly braided and rested to the side and down across her simple, modest gown. It rose and fell with each breath, as did her lovely bosom. Pouty lips of a dusky rose, though unsmiling, were in want of kissing. She was exactly the woman he wanted by his side, but he knew it wasn't going to be easy to convince her of that. He glanced over at Merry, who was perfection in every way, from her hair to her dress to her sweet demeanor. Most men would choose her over Isla, but not Aleck. It was Isla he had thought of almost daily since first meeting her a few months ago. He was determined to make her his before their visit was done. Isla must have felt his eyes on her because she turned and challenged him with her glare.

"Why do ye stare at me?" she asked.

"Do I need reason to wish to bathe my eyes in your beauty?" He thought himself quite clever, thinking of those poetic words on the spot. Isla, however, seemed unimpressed. "I'm nay a bad man, Isla." Why he felt the need to defend himself was unknown, for the words left his mouth before he had a chance to stop them.

She gave him an appraising look. "That remains to be seen."

ALECK SAW KAT and Nick settled in to their chamber and then Merry, who in true Merry form happily bounced into the room, closing the door behind her. That left him alone with Isla, who was appearing quite uncomfortable. Her eyes darted around the passageway, looking at everything but him, until she seemed to have settled on studying the ceiling. He was enjoying this. He could very easily have asked one of the servants to show them to their rooms, but then he would have lost out on the pleasure of seeing Isla Mackall squirm.

"Isla, your chamber will be here." He escorted her to a door a bit further removed from the others and opened it for her to pass through, then followed her in. The room had a decently large bed along one side and a fireplace along another. He was pleased to see that the servants had lit the fire so the room was warm and comfortable for her. The window was covered now against the chill of the evening, but he knew that in the morning she would be able to look out and see the sunrise. If she was an early riser, that is. Aleck suddenly had a vision of her early in the morning, her face soft from sleep and wrapped in his arms. He had to shake that vision.

"If there's anything ye should need, day or night, I'm right across the hall from ye." His voice came out huskier than usual, he hoped she wouldn't notice.

She closed her eyes and took in a good deep breath. "Aleck, I'm perfectly capable of taking care of meself. I dinnae believe I'll need yer help today, tomorrow or ever. Now, if ye'll excuse me, ye shouldnae be in here and I'd like to rest."

"Of course." He took a moment more to study her face then turned to leave. He wanted to say more, but thought better of it. Let her believe what she liked, but Aleck's plans to woo her would change her mind.

He softly closed the door and returned to his daily duties. He'd see them all again later at the evening meal, but for now he was the laird of this castle and there was much to be done.

CHAPTER 7

O VER THE NEXT few weeks, Isla did her best to keep watch over Merry, never allowing her to be alone with Aleck for more than even a few moments. She didn't trust him, although he'd given her no reason to feel this way and in fact, if she really gave it some thought, she'd realize that she was the one who seemed to be spending the most time alone with him. He always seemed to find her, no matter where she went. It had become almost intolerable for her. There were all these feelings for him that she didn't wish to have and it angered her. She became either an unintelligible mess when they were alone or she let the anger she was feeling towards herself spill out in rudeness towards Aleck. He'd been a perfect gentlemen, never even so much as touching her. It was her traitorous body that was the problem. Try as she might, she simply couldn't stop the butterflies, from invading her belly every time she saw him. The control she'd shown over the past few years in every aspect of her life was beginning to unravel and it was most unsettling. It was easier to concentrate on Merry and remember that she was the one who should be matched with Aleck. Even still, she felt the need to chaperone them, and so she now found herself tagging along behind them as they made their way to the garden, which Merry was very excited to see.

Aleck stopped, turning to wait for Isla as she marched up to the two of them. "Would ye care to join us?" he asked, with a smug grin on his lips.

"I believe I shall," Isla replied.

"Good. Merry has been telling me that she loves flowers and I believe I've some beauties to show her. What about ye? Do ye enjoy flowers?"

"As much as anyone," she replied.

"She does, if the right person gives them to her," Merry added and then seemed to wish she hadn't spoken.

Isla stopped and glared at her.

"Is something wrong?" Aleck asked.

"Nay. My sister doesnae ken what she speaks of, 'tis all."

"I'm sorry, Isla." Merry hugged her sister's arm.

Aleck was happy to see Isla respond in kind. Something was amiss with her. He had no idea what it could be, but was determined to discover the reason for her ill temper. He offered his arm to Merry, who eagerly took it. He did the same with Isla and was quite sure she'd refuse, but she surprised him by gingerly placing her hand on his arm as if she were afraid to touch him. He led them down the pathways that were woven through the beds of flowers, stopping at a particularly beautiful rose bush.

"I love roses," Merry said, inhaling the scent of the nearest blossom.

Aleck removed his dirk and cut each sister a blossom, carefully removing the thorns before presenting them. Merry immediately stuck her nose into the heavily scented flower, inhaling the delicious aroma. Isla barely glanced at hers, instead letting the hand that held the rose fall by her side. There was a sadness about her. A sadness that she covered up with anger and disinterest, but a sadness that, at the moment, was very apparent to him.

She cleared her throat. "Merry, I'm feeling tired. I believe I'll go lie down for a bit. Ye'll be fine with Laird Sinclair." She turned to Aleck. Her eyes downcast. "Thank ye fer showing us yer garden."

"'Twas me pleasure, Isla." He had barely finished speaking before she was walking away from him at a rather fast clip. Both he and Merry watched until she was out of sight.

"So much lavender!" Merry exclaimed heading straight towards it.

"I believe yer trying to distract me," Aleck noted.

Merry furrowed her brow. "What do ye mean? I only wished

to see the flowers up close."

"I don't imagine you'd like to tell me what bothers Isla."

She glanced everywhere but at him. He gently placed a finger beneath her chin and tipped it up so he could see her eyes.

"I cannae. Isla has sworn me to secrecy and I cannae betray her trust."

"I respect yer loyalty to yer sister," Aleck assured her.

"Isla will have to be the one to tell ye."

"Of course. I dinnae wish to jeopardize yer relationship with her. I'll ask her meself."

"Isla is a good sister," Merry said. "She's going through a difficult time, but she hasn't always been this way, ye ken." Her eyes pleaded with him to understand, so he gave a short nod in reply. Merry seemed satisfied with that and her smile returned. She turned back to the lavender, inhaling the soft scent and running her hands along the buds waving in the breeze.

Aleck wondered if he would be fighting a losing battle by pursuing Isla. Perhaps it would be easier to let her go and to turn his attention to Merry. He dismissed that thought as soon as it formed. Isla was the one he wanted. He'd known it from the first moment he laid eyes on her. He'd give it more time and hope she would eventually let her guard down and allow him to see who she really was. He believed if she did he'd find the woman he'd always hoped would someday be his wife.

ONCE OUT OF the garden, Isla ran. She had to get as far away from here as she could. Her memories were playing tricks on her, at once so real and yet blurry, like seeing a landscape through a fog. The edges were soft and indistinct. The sounds so distant, as to barely be heard. There had been a different man in a different garden, handing her a rose and smiling at her. She thought back to the small box in her room at Dunnet Head. Though its once velvety soft red petals were now black and brittle with age, that rose held the memory of a spring day, of a voice that was fading away. For the last few months she had strained to hear it, tried hard to see that smile in her dreams, but both were lost to the passing of time.

Unsure of where to go or what to do, she continued to run. She ran from her past, ran from her feelings, ran from Aleck. She ran until she couldn't run any more. Doubled over and gasping for breath, she stopped at the crest of the hill and struggled to bring those memories back into focus, to find that pain that meant he was still with her. But it did not come. The tears did not threaten. Instead she collapsed against a tree, breathing heavy from her run, and stared at the horizon with the flower still clutched in her hand.

NICK WAS WAITING for Aleck by the fire in the great hall. As Aleck approached, he handed him a quaich of whisky, which he happily accepted. "Where's Kat?" Aleck asked.

"She's resting in our chamber," Nick answered. "She'll be down for the evening meal. Did ye enjoy spending time with Isla and Merry this day."

"Aye." Aleck said, but then corrected himself. "It wasnae as I wished it to be."

"What do ye mean?"

Aleck thought about how to explain things to Nick. He hoped his friend could enlighten him as to what was wrong. "Merry was most happy to spend time with me, but Isla only came along to make sure I behaved myself with Merry. She doesnae seem happy to be here."

Nick took another sip of his whisky and stared into the glass as though it held the answer. With a deep breath he looked up at Aleck and said, "I willnae lie to ye. She doesnae wish to be here."

43

Aleck was taken aback. What could he say to that? Had he imagined her response to him at the wedding? He thought back to that night, that moment alone with her in the hallway. He thought about the way she felt in his arms, the way she responded to his kiss. Yes, he had tried to annoy her by dancing with Merry, but surely she knew where his true interest lie. Perhaps he had misread the entire situation. Perhaps she was angry with him or hated him for playing with her emotions. This is not what he expected when Nick wrote to say they were all coming for a visit.

"Kat and I believe ye two would be a good match," Nick said.

"I believed so too," Aleck replied. He would need to be a man about this. If she hated him so much he would have to let her go. That thought was followed by pain in his chest, but there was no way he would let Nick see that he was affected.

"Isla will come around. She has never been one who likes being told what to do. She prefers to have a choice."

"Then why did ye nae give her one?" Aleck did not like the idea of Isla being manipulated into something. Nick did not seem like the kind of brother that would trick his sister into marrying someone, especially since their clans were already closely aligned.

Nick, again, looked thoughtfully into his whisky. There must be something more to this.

"Merry hinted that something had happened to Isla. Something that made her quite unhappy," Aleck prompted.

"They dinnae speak of it." There was pain in his friend's voice. "I was lost in the future for a few years and something happened while I was gone. They all seem to think that if no one speaks of it, she will get past it. But to my eyes, my sister is not herself. She always had her own opinion about everything and it was good fun to argue with her about the color of the sky, or anything else, while we were growing up. But she is different now. She argues with me fer certain, but it is not the same." Aleck could see the pain and worry in his friend's face. "Merry and our mother noticed that she showed a bit of interest in ye. She seemed for a moment to be her former self. I hoped that by spending time with ye, she would get beyond the pain of the past and find a way to be happy, that's all."

"Then we are faced with a dilemma. If she willnae speak of it with ye, chances of her telling me what has happened are nae good. I care fer yer sister, Nick. I do want her to be me wife, but I dinnae know if I can help her through this." Aleck felt the wind rush out of him. His whole life he had been brought up to lead the clan. To help the people he cared about in the castle and the village through the tough times. He had always found a way, but now with this woman, the only woman he could imagine by his side, he was lost and had no way forward.

"Don't give up." Nick placed his hand on Aleck's shoulder. "She's worth the trouble ye'll go through to have her."

"I ken it. I will continue to try."

Nick seemed pleased with that answer. In a moment, gone was the worried brother and in his place was the smiling, relaxed man Aleck knew so well. Nick finished his drink and smiled, "Have Merry help ye."

"Aye," Aleck laughed. "Isla doesnae wish me to be left alone with Merry. She has made that abundantly clear." He shook his head in wonder at how Isla could possibly think he had any interest in Merry.

"Kat and I will be leaving for Edinburgh soon enough. We must have a good reason for Merry to stay behind. Isla willnae leave her here alone with ye."

"How is it that she's come to think so poorly of me?"

"'Tis nae that she thinks poorly of ye. I believe that while she says she isnae interested in ye, she doesnae wish Merry to be either. Ye see, she says one thing and does another. 'Tis quite confusing."

"That it is." Aleck considered his options. Then inspiration struck. "I will plan a feast."

Nick barked a laugh, "What will ye celebrate?"

"When ye return with Kat, we will celebrate my sister! Merry can help me with the plans." Aleck considered the plan and liked it very much. He was very excited to have his sister back after a lifetime apart. He should have thought of this before, but now the celebration would serve a dual purpose.

"I believe that will work."

Aleck felt hopeful. If he could convince Merry to help him, then perhaps he had a chance. It was the best he could do and hoped it would work. He'd find Merry and hopefully be able to speak with her alone.

"So, ye wish me to help ye make Isla jealous." Merry gazed off into the distance, standing with her hands on her hips and tapping her foot on the ground. He found her out in the garden helping the cook gather herbs for tonight's meal and chatting happily about gardening techniques. Merry, it seemed, could talk to anyone about anything at any time and appear to thoroughly enjoy every moment of it.

"Well, will ye do it?" Aleck asked.

"Aye. I'll help ye," she nodded, "I want Isla to be happy again and I believe yer the one for her." She peeked around Aleck. "Here she comes. Mayhap we should start now." Without any warning, Merry wrapped her arms around Aleck's waist and gazed up into his face.

Taken off guard, Aleck hesitated only a moment before wrapping his arms around her. He felt guilty, but this was his plan after all, he'd best play along.

"What do ye think yer doing? Dinnae touch her." Isla stormed up to them, face reddened in anger.

Aleck released Merry.

"Isla, why are ye so upset?" Merry asked. She was quite a good actress. "We were just enjoying each other's company."

"Merry, I dinnae believe Ma would be happy to ken ye were throwing yerself at Laird Sinclair. 'Tis nae right. And ye…" She turned on him with fire in her eyes. "Ye shouldnae take advantage of Merry. She's a good lass."

Aleck hid his smile behind his hand as he stared down at the ground. "I beg yer pardon, Isla. I dinnae ken what came over me."

"Well, whatever it was, dinnae let it happen again." She grabbed Merry by the arm and dragged her away.

"Isla stop! I can walk on me own." Merry glanced back over her shoulder and winked at Aleck, who had all he could do not to laugh out loud.

CHAPTER 8

"ARE YE SURE ye dinnae wish to join us, Merry?" Kat asked. They were mounted and ready to leave for Edinburgh.

"Nae. I wish to help Aleck prepare for the feast. He is in sore need of help," Merry replied.

Isla rolled her eyes. That wasn't exactly true. Aleck had a host of servants who seemed quite good at their tasks. He had announced his intention to host a feast for Kat and invite the neighboring clans, of course Merry jumped at the chance to help. The next two weeks would involve writing letters, planning menus and decorating the castle. All things Isla hated. If it wasn't clear already, this whole process would make everyone see that she would be a terrible wife to a laird.

"What of ye, Isla?" Nick asked.

"I'll stay with Merry. She may need me help and I can keep a close watch on her." Although Isla thought it a good idea for her sister to marry Aleck, she didn't wish her to be put in a compromising position by being left alone with him. "'Tis best if I stay."

"As you wish," Nick said, winking at Kat.

"What are ye up to, brother?" Isla asked, eyes slanted and chin raised.

"Nary a thing, lass. Can a man nay wink at his wife?" he chuckled.

Isla thought otherwise. She knew exactly how Nick and Kat felt about her staying here with Aleck. "Mayhap ye should stay here as well. Protect yer sisters."

"From what?" Aleck had silently crept up behind them, causing Isla to jump.

"Ye've nothing to fear from Aleck," Kat assured her. "He'll be a perfect gentleman or he'll have Nick to answer to when we return."

Isla's heart continued to beat loudly in her ears and her hands suddenly felt sweaty. He was standing more than a foot away from her, but it still seemed too close.

"Just what do ye think I'll be up to?" Aleck directed his question to Isla.

"Something, I'm sure." Her look told him she was thinking about what she'd seen the other day.

"'Tis vague. Do ye have something more exact that ye'd wish to share." Isla could feel her face reddening and rather than withstand more teasing from all assembled, she turned and stormed off holding on to her last shred of dignity.

ALECK COULDN'T HELP but chuckle as Isla raced away. "I fear yer sister doesnae care for me."

"She's her own worst enemy," Nick said. "Hopefully she'll come around while we're away. I believe ye've yer work cut out for ye."

"I believe I'm up to the challenge," Aleck said. "Merry will help me, won't ye?" Aleck glanced at Merry, who loved being in on his plot to win Isla over.

She nodded her head. "Ye can count on me," she replied.

"Shall we get started, Nick? I can hardly wait to see Edinburgh."

His sister was becoming impatient. "Why are ye in such a hurry to see Edinburgh?" Aleck asked. "Didnae ye live there growing up?"

"She wishes to see it the way it is in this time," Nick explained.

"Aye. I've seen it in the future and, as an archeologist, I'm curious to see it now, with me own eyes."

Aleck loved his sister. He'd not known her at all as he grew into a man, but to find her after all those years was more than he could have hoped for. She was everything he'd thought she would be and he was enjoying the chance to get to know her. "Well, be on yer way then and hurry back. I want ye back here for the feast I've planned in yer honor."

"We'll do our best," Nick assured him as they turned away.

He watched them until they were out of sight. "Shall we?" He presented his arm to Merry, who took it with a giggle. "We've much to do, if our plan is to succeed."

Isla was furious with herself for letting Aleck Sinclair get under her skin. She prided herself on never allowing her enemies to cause her to lose focus. But Aleck Sinclair wasn't her enemy. Perhaps that was the problem. If he was, she'd surely have better luck dealing with him. He'd been nothing if not kind and gentlemanly to both she and Merry since they'd arrived, with mayhap the exception of the time she'd found Merry in his arms. Although, truth be told, when she'd approached them it appeared that Merry had thrown herself at him and he'd merely responded in kind. She had no reason at all to be angry with him. Nothing except the fact that he made her heart beat faster and her breath come in small gasps whenever he got too close. Keeping him at arms' length would be her best bet. And why was it that every time she saw him with her sister she wanted to scream? She, herself, knew Merry was the better choice to be his wife. Isla had no intentions of marrying now or ever. She had no desire to be a wife, a mother, or the lady of this castle. She'd wanted such things once a lifetime ago, but not any longer.

Glancing back over her shoulder, she was just in time to see Aleck and Merry, arm-in-arm and laughing at some joke, following along behind her. They were probably laughing at her, she thought. This was intolerable. For the hundredth time she wished she was back home with her Ma at Dunnet Head. She quickly veered away from the castle, heading through the courtyard as if that had been her plan all along. She ducked into the farrier's stall and tucked herself among the tools hanging on the wall. She peeked around the corner to watch Aleck and Merry as they sauntered into the castle.

"Can I help ye, lass?" Isla jumped. The farrier appeared from the opposite side of the stall where he'd been hammering away at a piece of molten metal.

"Nay," she said stepping toward him, she had to think of a reason for what she was doing in here. "I was…just…curious to see what all the noise was in here."

The farrier cocked his head, then smiled at her. He was wearing a leather apron, with soot covering everything from his elbows down. His bright blue eyes shined through the soot she could see caked in every wrinkle that surrounded them. "I thought ye may be hiding from someone the way that ye've tucked yerself in behind the wall." He chuckled to himself, "If yer really interested, I'm working on a sword for one of the men." He waved her over to the forge where the fire was burning bright.

She was interested. "A sword. May I see?" Suddenly all thoughts of Aleck and Merry were banished.

He held up the unfinished sword blade for her to see. "I've more work to do on it before I'm done." He stretched and cracked his neck, obviously relieving some of the strain from wielding the heavy hammer he used to pound the metal into the shape he wanted. His massive arms were well muscled from years of plying his trade. "Here's another I've been working on." He placed the unfinished sword back on the anvil and picked up another from beside the work bench. "Here ye go, lass." He handed it to Isla.

She gripped it in her hand, feeling the perfect balance and weight of it before handing it back to him with a nod of approval. She then took a moment to glance around the space. The heat from the fire permeated the small but functional area, along with the smell of smoke, iron and sweat. She saw a few stalls with horses patiently waiting to be shod, as well as all of the tools of this farrier's trade. Horseshoes hung from the wall, along with a bellows for stoking the fire, a water trough for quenching the molten metal and a whet stone for grinding and sharpening. She was suitably impressed.

"If I brought ye my sword, could ye sharpen it fer me?" Isla asked.

"Ye've a sword?" he seemed only slightly incredulous.

"Aye."

"Whatever for?" She could see his curiosity had been piqued.

"Can a lady nae enjoy a bit of swordplay?" she asked, expecting him to say swordplay was for the men and nae lady should ever use a sword, but he surprised her.

"Bring it. I'd be happy to sharpen it fer ye." He went to work the bellows until the fire grew large and filled the air with snaps and cracks, then he picked up the sword from his work bench and thrust it into the flame until it glowed.

"Thank ye," she said, ducking out of the stall. She could hear the pounding of his hammer all the way to the castle doors.

THE SOUNDS OF Merry's laughter could be heard coming from the great hall. Isla quietly entered, not sure what she was expecting to find, but hoping it wasn't Merry snuggled in Aleck's arms once again.

"Isla, there ye be!" Aleck called.

"Join us," Merry added. "We were discussing the plans for Kat's feast."

Isla approached them, not terribly interested in helping.

"We're planning the meal. Would ye like to help us decide?" she asked.

Isla thought of the feasts they had planned together at home. Endless hours discussing how to cook meat and which vegetables were ready to harvest. But the kitchen wasn't for her. She preferred to be outdoors in the fresh air and did her best to avoid the more womanly duties when at Dunnet Head. "Ye ken I'm nae verra good…"

"Isla, I'll not hear another word," Merry said, interrupting her. "Ye ken just as much as Aleck and I."

She couldn't really argue with Merry, because she was right, but she *was* pretty sure she knew more than Aleck.

"Ye like to eat, dinnae ye?" Aleck asked, a look of mischief on his handsome face.

"Aye," she replied with reluctance, not wishing him to be right.

"Then yer just as qualified to plan the meal as I am." He straightened, crossing his arms in front of his chest.

Isla couldn't help but smile, but as soon as it appeared that Aleck had noticed, she wiped it from her face.

He leaned across the table towards her, "Why do ye nae smile more? Yer pretty when ye smile."

"And I'm nae pretty when I'm nae smiling?" she asked, feeling quite insulted by his words.

The look on Aleck's face almost brought another, bigger grin to Isla's lips, but she kept it in check.

"'Tis nae what I meant," Aleck quickly corrected.

She enjoyed seeing him squirm and so she continued to argue.

"'Tis what ye said," she pointed out, her feelings vindicated.

Merry hadn't uttered a word, instead her gaze flew from one to the other as they spoke.

"Isla, yer purposely being difficult," Aleck said, his voice defensive and decidedly louder. "I didnae mean to insult ye."

"Aye, but ye did and ye did it again now," she yelled back.

"Again?" the man looked truly lost. Isla hadn't enjoyed anything quite as much as this in a long, long time.

She stood and leaned across the table until they were practically nose to nose, "Ye called me difficult. So, I'm nae pretty *and* I'm difficult." She stood up with her hands on her hips and continued, her voice too sweet to be sincere. "Thank ye so verra much for yer observations, Laird Sinclair. I dinnae believe I can stay and help ye with yer feast." Once again she stormed away, but before she had even left the room she regretted her actions. This was becoming a not very attractive habit. She was supposed to be pleasant. She was supposed to remember that Aleck was not her enemy. But honestly, she had never been any good at doing the things that she, as a lady, was supposed to do.

There were better ways to spend her time than planning food and helping with invitations for the feast. She had a sword that needed to be sharpened and, as soon as it was, she intended to do something else ladies were not supposed to do.

"Well, that didnae go verra well," Aleck said as he watched Isla's back receding from view.

"It didnae," Merry observed.

Aleck wiped his hand down his face in disbelief, "I cannae seem to say or do anything right when she's near." He was dumbfounded.

"Do ye nae have much experience wooing the lasses, Aleck?" Merry teased.

"I do and I would prove it to her, if she'd let me." Aleck sat up a bit straighter and tried to look stern, but inside he was off-kilter.

"Ye can practice on me," Merry shrugged. "If ye wish to make her jealous and not just angry with ye."

"I dinnae need practice." He was not a lad of twelve, though he certainly sounded like one. He was a laird, a man in charge, he had been approached by many a father hoping to make a good match and form an alliance. But he wanted to marry someone that would challenge him. He really wondered what he could have been thinking. "I've never met a woman quite so…"

"Difficult. I believe that's the word ye used before."

"Aye. And 'tis what she is."

"Mayhap 'tis what ye like about her."

Aleck thought about that for a minute. She wasnae a typical lass. She was quite beautiful in his eyes, although she did her best to hide it beneath drab clothing, doing nothing to enhance her natural beauty. She had a sharp tongue and a sharp wit, which she seemed to take great pleasure in using against him. And while he wished she'd be softer where he was concerned, he liked the spark he saw flash in her eyes when she was angry. It told of a deeper passion waiting to be uncovered. Hopefully he would be the man to uncover it.

"Aleck, where have ye gone off to?" Merry asked, a knowing smile lighting her lips.

"I'm right here," Aleck said, thankful that the table would hide his aroused state. He cleared his throat and tried to think of anything besides an uncovered Isla in his arms. "Shall we continue?"

They were joined by several servants and the castle cook. Aleck and Merry told them of their plans for the feast and Merry offered to help in any way necessary to make sure that Kat's feast was perfect. Aleck was impressed with her ability to take charge of a group of strangers and have them all ready and willing to do her bidding. She would surely be an asset to any laird in need of a lady.

CHAPTER 9

W HAT HAD STARTED out as fun teasing had turned into something altogether different. She'd been hurt when Aleck called her difficult, although she knew deep down that she deserved it. She *was* difficult and she didn't care if he liked it or not.

After leaving her sword with the farrier, she paced back and forth in the garden in frustration. Her mind was reeling. Conflicting feelings about Aleck and her unwanted attraction to him were making her life extremely difficult. And why was it that every time she saw him with Merry, jealousy reared its ugly head. She wanted Merry to be with him, didn't she? That was a question she was having a harder and harder time answering. She stopped her pacing. At home when she was feeling this way, she'd grab her sword and march herself down to the practice field where she'd grab a warrior to spar with. She always felt better afterwards when her arms were heavy from wielding her sword and her mind was finally clear of whatever had been bothering her. She decided even if she couldn't fight, she'd go to the one place she always felt comfortable.

Isla marched out to the practice field to watch then men practicing, all the while wishing she could get her hands on a sword and get rid of some of the anger she was feeling.

"Would ye care to join us?" Aleck's captain, whom she recognized, approached her. She cocked her head slightly, unsure she'd heard correctly.

"How did ye ken?" she asked.

"The scowl yer wearing on yer face gave ye away. Ye look as if ye'd like to soundly bash something or someone." He smiled reassuringly at her.

"Aye. I do feel that way." She returned his smile. Finally, someone understood how she felt.

"Come then. I'll spar with ye." He motioned her to join him.

As excited as she was to be invited, she was disappointed she wouldn't be able to. "But I dinnae have me sword."

"Ye can use one of our practice swords. It will keep me from harm," he teased. "I'll do the same."

"Alright. Thank ye." She was incredibly grateful and very excited. Her breathing quickened as did her heartbeat and this time, she was happy to note, it wasn't because of Aleck Sinclair.

"I be Taegen Creag, Laird Sinclair's captain." He handed her a wooden sword and took one for himself.

"I'm Isla Mackall," she replied.

He bowed slightly to her with a flourish of his arm, making her smile.

Facing an opponent she'd never met before would be new for her. She hadn't had that opportunity to this point. At home, she knew all the men and they her, so this would be a challenge of her skills. She assumed Taegen wasn't expecting much from her, so she did her best to surprise him.

The wooden sword felt strange in her hand, but after taking a moment for a few practice swings, she began to feel the balance and movement she was searching for. Taegen handed her a targe, which she slid into place on her arm, then took her position across from him. She immediately went on the offensive.

He jumped back as she swung her sword at him, holding up his targe to deflect her strike. "I like the way ye used the element of surprise. Ye willnae surprise me again, lass."

Isla's eyes flashed and she put all her weight behind every thrust and slash, imagining Aleck Sinclair was her target. Taegen was quick, but he didnae engage her in battle by returning her assault.

"That's right lass. Relax and remember to breathe. Ye'll do better if you're calm and in control of yer emotions. Keep yer elbows bent and your sword in a middle position." She circled him, listening to his encouraging words. His voice soothed her and any frustration she'd felt when they'd started had melted away. For his part, Teagen was merely in defensive mode, she assumed because he thought he might hurt her. He allowed her to wack away at him until she was out of breath and felt much better than she had in the garden. In fact, she couldn't stop smiling.

"Ye show much promise," Taegen said as he took her sword and targe.

"Thank ye. Back home I'm allowed to practice with the men." He didn't seem surprised to hear it.

"If ye like, I can give ye some pointers tomorrow."

"I'd like that," she responded, trying not to appear too excited at the prospect of doing what she loved most in the world. She could hardly believe her good fortune.

"There are a few areas where ye can use some improvement. The first being to control yer anger. Ye'll always be at a disadvantage if ye go into a fight filled with ire.

Isla laughed. "I ken it. I was imaging yer laird standing there."

Taegen didn't seem too terribly surprised by this, instead he tipped his head, gazing into her eyes as if he could see into her very soul. "He's done something to anger ye?"

"'Twas something he said," she replied.

Taegen nodded his head in understanding. "I'll be happy to be a stand in for the laird if it will keep ye from murdering him."

"No need to worry. I could never do that." She found herself laughing, something she hadn't done a lot of since arriving at Sinclair Castle. In fact, this had been the most comfortable she'd felt in quite some time and that made her ecstatic.

"'Tis good to hear. So tomorrow then?"

"I'll be here," Isla said, standing tall. She watched as Taegen's eyes looked past her and turned to see what he was looking at.

"There ye be," Merry said, hurrying to her side. "I was worried about ye."

"Nae need to worry, Taegen has been sparring with me, 'tis all."

Merry glanced at the tall, handsome Taegen and blushed. He bowed his head slightly in her direction.

"This is my sister, Merry." Isla watched as her sister grew more and more uncomfortable standing there.

"Good day to ye," Merry mumbled.

"Good day, Merry. I'm pleased to meet ye."

Taegen's icy blue eyes were fixed on Merry, as he brushed his long black locks from his face. Isla had to admit she enjoyed watching her sister squirm for once. She was always so at ease with everyone she met, including men. Something about Taegen was causing an awkwardness in Merry she'd never seen before.

"Ye should join us tomorrow," Isla said.

"I couldnae," Merry blushed a darker shade of red.

"Of course, ye could."

"Isla, ye ken I'm nae good with a sword," Merry whispered, letting her glance stray to Taegen.

"Ye could watch," Isla said. "Please. Ye always say ye want to spend time with me." She'd learned a thing or two from Merry about cajoling someone into doing something they didn't want to do.

Isla observed that Merry couldn't stop looking at Taegen, who seemed unaware of her distress.

"I'll leave ye then. I've more work to attend to," Taegen said, bowing to both of them. "I hope ye'll join us tomorrow."

Merry gave a quick wave goodbye as he strode off to join his men.

"Ye like him, dinnae ye?" Isla asked.

"He's so verra handsome. I like his eyes," Merry said, her voice soft and dreamy.

"Mayhap tomorrow ye can get to know him better," Isla suggested.

"Nae. I cannae," Merry's voice conveyed her disappointment as she very obviously followed Taegen with her eyes as he walked away.

"And why nae?" Isla asked with a teasing lilt to her voice.

"I'm helping Aleck. I've nae time." The look of disappointment on Merry's face spoke volumes.

Isla felt a momentary jolt of jealousy, forgetting for a moment it had been her thought that Merry should marry Aleck, but if Merry liked this Taegen better, so be it.

"Merry, what about spending time together?" Isla gave her best sad pout.

"I'll come for a little while," Merry said, her eyes bright once again and the disappointment gone from her tone.

"Good." Isla smiled to herself. This would be fun. She was tired of everyone always trying to match her with Aleck. It was her turn to be a matchmaker. Now maybe Merry would see what it felt like. Merry spent much of her time making everyone else happy. Isla wanted her to know how it felt to be captivated by a handsome young man, much as she'd once been. For herself, she realized that where there had once been a sharp pain at her loss, there was now only a dull ache.

ALECK VOWED HE would do his best not to say things that upset Isla ever again and over the course of the next few days he succeeded. Today, however, he wouldn't be so lucky.

He'd been locked up in his office for hours tending to the affairs of the castle. In fact, for the past few days he'd been busy going over his accounts and helping Merry prepare for the feast. These were all things he relished doing. Being the laird of his clan was his greatest joy, but he really needed to get outside in the fresh air. To that end, Aleck walked to his window, which looked out over the practice field. His men were working hard out there and he decided he'd join them.

Grabbing his sword and targe he headed outside, ready to put in some work with his men. As he approached the practice field, he took a moment to observe them. He was proud of this group of men. He knew he could count on them in any battle that may occur. His captain, Taegen, was in the midst of the others with his back to Aleck, battling with an unknown opponent. Glancing around, Aleck noticed Merry watching the men and cheering from just beyond the field. She was focused on Taegen, which made Aleck smile. Taegen was his best warrior and a great captain. He took a personal interest in each of the men, working with each one to develop their skills. The other warrior was getting in some good hits with Taegen's encouragement. As Taegen spun out of the way, Aleck was shocked to see Isla was the warrior he'd been sparring with.

"What's going on here?" Aleck roared, bringing everyone's sparring to a halt. He marched over to Taegen and Isla. "What is she doing here?" he said, speaking to Taegen.

Taegen opened his mouth to speak, but Isla beat him to it.

"I'm here to practice," Isla said with a bit of challenge in her voice.

Aleck furrowed his brow and looked back at Taegen. "'Tis nae a place for a lady." He realized as soon as the words left his mouth that he'd made yet another verbal blunder.

"Then mayhap I'm nae a lady." Isla raised her voice and appeared to be fighting mad.

Aleck narrowed his eyes and glared at his men. "Leave! Practice is over!"

The men disappeared with remarkable speed.

Merry went to stand by Taegen's side, apparently to get a better view of the battle that was about to take place.

"'Tis nae what I meant," Aleck blundered. "I'm sorry, but do ye see any other ladies of the castle here?"

"I dinnae. And if their laird is as daft an idjit as he appears, then I can understand why they would stay away."

Aleck took a moment before responding. He knew he was treading on thin ice and needed to be careful. Isla stood before him with fire in her eyes, breathing hard and looking a glorious, disheveled mess with her hair coming loose from her braid and her face and clothing covered in dirt. *My god,* he thought, *this woman is not a simple lady of the castle. She's a warrior.* He could feel his heart pounding in his chest, everything around him seemed to disappear and all he could see was Isla. There will never be another woman like her and he didn't want to say something that would destroy any chance he may have with her.

"Isla, I'm trying to protect ye. Ye could be hurt," Aleck pleaded his case, his voice softening as he did so.

"I dinnae need yer protection, nor do I want it. I'm perfectly capable of taking care of meself. I practice with the men at home all the time. Merry will tell ye."

She stood with her hands on her hips, eyes alight with fire and Aleck thought once again she was the most beautiful woman he'd ever laid eyes on. He knew if he continued on this path that it would be a long time before he was back in her good favor.

"If ye insist on doing this, I will be yer opponent," Aleck said, pleased with the surprise on Isla's face.

She regained her composure and nodded, glancing at Taegen and Merry, who didn't appear that they would relinquish their prime positions on the sidelines.

"Remember what I've told ye," Taegen said.

"How long have ye been allowing her to fight?" Aleck couldn't believe his ears.

"A few days," Taegen replied.

Aleck could't believe his ears. He looked to the sky, trying to regain his composure. "I spend far too much time with the ledgers."

"It sounds to me as if ye could use some practice. I'd be happy to give ye some pointers," Isla said, obviously trying to provoke him.

"Ye believe ye can give me some pointers, lass? I believe ye'll find that in any encounter with me on or off the field, I have far more experience than ye and I'll gladly show ye."

Feeling he'd gotten the better of her that time, he was surprised to find her finger poking him in the chest as she glared up into his face and snarled, "Well then, there's only one way to settle this."

They were standing toe to toe now, glaring at one another.

"Aye. Yer right." Aleck scooped her into his arms and before she could protest, kissed her soundly on the lips, receiving a resounding slap across the face as his reward for such insolence. She then stomped on his foot for good measure before marching away.

This woman was going to be the death of him. It was more than apparent that she disliked him, perhaps even hated him, and yet he wanted her. He was an idjit! He does one thing that makes her smile and then ruins it by immediately doing another that makes her hate him. He should just resign himself to life with some boring little wife. Things would be so much easier if he'd found Merry even half as appealing as Isla, she'd be so much easier to woo. He glanced Merry's way and saw that she was deep in conversation with Taegen. *No, I can see I'm already too late for that, too.*

Merry finished her conversation with Taegen and walked over to Aleck. Taking him by the arm she guided him away from the practice field. "Maybe you do need a few tips in wooing," she said.

Aleck shook his head, sweet little Merry was right. He needed all the help he could get where Isla was concerned.

"At home, 'tis common knowledge that Isla practices with the men. Ma wishes she wouldnae. She believes she'll never find a husband who wants a warrior wife and that she'd be better served learning needlecraft and how to manage a castle."

"I'm sure Isla must hate that," he chuckled.

"She does, but she kens we all only want the best for her. Still, we cannae stop her from her daily practice. She seems to need it." Merry was quiet for a moment and he wondered when the fighting practice had started. "The only one who could stop her is Nick and he doesnae believe there's any harm in allowing it."

"What do the men think of this?"

"They are impressed with her skills and dedication. Any one of them would be more than happy to have her fighting by their side in battle."

"She's good then?"

"Verra."

Aleck smiled to himself, of course she was good. Anyone could see that.

Merry rubbed his arm as if he were a wee bairn who needed comforting. "As for Taegen, dinnae be too hard on him. He saw Isla's interest and didnae believe there was any harm in letting her practice her skills as long as he was the one she worked with."

Aleck felt a pang of jealousy. He'd been so wrapped up in castle business that he hadn't known she was practicing with the men. Why hadn't she come to him? Because he would have done exactly what he'd done this morning. She knew it and bypassed him. "I must apologize to her. I shouldnae have kissed her like that out in the open. 'Twas disrespectful."

"Let me speak with her. She'll be too angry with ye still. Ye may not leave that conversation with yer head still attached to yer body."

She left him to find Isla. He could kick himself. He may have ruined any chance he could have had with her.

CHAPTER 10

"**Y**E SHOULDNAE BE so hard on him," Merry said.

"And why would that be?" Isla asked.

"Ye ken ye like him."

"I dinnae." All she'd been able to think about since the scene on the practice field was that kiss. It was unexpected and in the heat of a passionate argument, but it singed her lips and burned its way deep into her soul.

"Of course ye do. Ye get jealous every time ye see us together." Merry stood opposite Isla in a private corner of the courtyard.

"'Tis nae true. I'm only trying to protect ye," Isla said, knowing it was true.

"There's nae need of that. He's always a gentleman with me. 'Tis ye he wants."

Isla didn't want to hear that. She shrugged her shoulders in defeat, "Well he cannae have me," she whispered. It would all be so much easier if they would leave her alone.

Isla felt Merry's hands on her shoulders. "Wouldnae ye like to be married, Isla?"

"Nae. I dinnae wish to marry and ye ken why."

"Derrick wouldnae wish ye to spend yer life alone."

"How do *ye* ken what he would or wouldnae wish?" she snapped. This was a subject best left alone.

"He was a good man, Isla. He loved ye so much and ye him, but he's nae longer here. He wouldnae want ye to live without love in yer life." Merry sounded so reasonable, but what did she know about it.

"I have love. I have our family. Ye all love me... or do ye?" She gazed at Merry, wondering if she was even loveable and dreading the thought that perhaps she wasn't. She scrubbed her hands though her hair, getting them caught in the knots that had formed when her braid began to come loose. She wanted to scream, but she wouldn't.

"Aye, we do," Merry assured her. "But dinnae ye wish to have someone to share yer life with?" Merry asked.

Isla was so tired of this conversation. She'd had it with her mother, her brothers, her sister, her brothers' wives and with practically everyone in the village. Everyone right down to the innkeeper and his daughter seemed to know what was best for her. After hearing that she had no intention of marrying, they'd sadly shake their heads disappointed they hadn't been the one to convince her to change her mind. They didn't know the real reason for her reluctance to fall in love and marry. If they did, perhaps they'd leave her alone.

"Dinnae ye get lonely?"

"Everyone gets lonely." She wasn't about to fall into Merry's trap. Of course she was lonely. The only man she'd ever loved had been taken from her and with him went all her hopes, her dreams of a home of her own and bairns to love. These constant reminders that Derrick was gone were unbearable. "Please stop it, Merry! If one more person tells me what I should do and how I should feel, I'll send meself to the nearest nunnery to escape this unending stream of good intentions you are all killing me with!"

Tears formed in Merry's eyes. "I'm so sorry, Isla. I didn't mean to upset ye so. I promise I'll nae mention it again."

Isla gathered her sister into her arms. "I'm the one who's sorry. I shouldnae have yelled at ye like that. I ken yer only wanting the best for me."

Merry stepped back and gazed into her sister's face. "Isla ye need to speak to Aleck. He wants to marry ye. Ye must tell him about Derrick. He'll nae doubt be disappointed, but he'll understand."

"'Tis none of his business," Isla said, but perhaps Merry was right. If she told him, he might leave her alone. And if he left her alone, it would mean he could marry Merry or someone else and nae give her another thought. Her heart hurt a bit at the thought of it, but she knew it was what must be done. Aleck was a good man and Merry would be the perfect wife for him. The sooner she expressed her feelings to him, the better.

The dining hall at Castle Sinclair was quiet this evening. Aleck, Merry and Isla were the only ones in attendance. Aleck made his apologies to Isla as soon as he saw her and she accepted, although she'd hardly spoken a word.

"Where is everyone tonight?" Merry asked.

"I dinnae always have a full hall at meal times," Aleck explained. "Me men have their own lives and families and those who arenae on duty, are most likely at home."

"What would ye do if we werenae here?"

"I'd eat in me chamber."

"Alone?" Merry seemed surprised by this.

"Aye. Alone." Seeing Merry's sad eyes staring at him, Aleck realized how pathetic that must sound. "I dinnae mind it. After a busy day, it is often a welcome respite."

"Oh," Merry said.

Aleck was sure he'd said the wrong thing again. He certainly didn't want the Mackall sisters to think he'd rather be eating in his room than here with them. "I do enjoy your company though."

"I'm glad of it," Merry said.

He hoped Isla didn't think it was Merry alone he was speaking to. "And you as well, Isla, of course."

She glanced up from the food she'd been staring at but hardly touched. "I'm sorry. I didnae hear what ye were saying."

"I was telling Merry how much I enjoy sharing a meal with the two of ye." His normal confident demeanor was being put to the test by this woman. He was beginning to think she really didn't care for him at all. She hardly gave him any notice and when she did… he wished he could read her mind. He'd love to know what was going on in there.

"Would ye excuse me, I'm suddenly feeling quite tired. I believe I'll retire for the evening."

"Of course," Aleck said, rising to pull Isla's chair out from the table.

"Thank ye." She walked away without looking back.

"Either I'm the most daft of men, or I seem to be chasing her away. She has used that excuse to escape me more than once now."

"'Tis nae just ye she wishes to escape. We had an argument earlier," Merry said, moving the food around on her trencher.

"Ye did? About what?" he asked.

"About ye," she seemed somewhat reluctant to admit this.

"What did she say?" He wasn't sure he wanted to know, but if he was going to solve the puzzle that was Isla, perhaps it would help.

"That she doesnae wish to marry ye."

Aleck would be lying if he said his feelings weren't hurt by this. In fact, he felt as if he'd been punched in the gut and he imagined it showed on his face, because Merry rushed to make him feel better.

"She said she didnae wish to marry anyone. 'Tis not only ye."

He was dumbfounded. "So, there's no hope then."

"I wouldnae say that. I still believe ye can win her over."

Aleck thought back on his earlier argument with Isla. He'd kissed her and that had been a mistake, but it certainly wasn't the reason she didn't wish to marry anyone. There was a sadness there. She tried to hide it, but it was there, nonetheless. He wished he knew what had happened to her. He wished she would confide in him. In order to do that, she had to trust him and so far he didn't think she trusted him one wee bit. His mind was racing. As the laird of his clan, one of his jobs was to solve their problems and if they didn't trust him, he wouldn't be able to help them. Somehow he needed to show Isla that he was trustworthy, that she could talk to him about anything. It occurred to him that what she wanted and needed more than anything was for him to see her as an equal.

She was a warrior at heart, just as he was. They had that in common.

"What are ye thinking, Aleck?" Merry asked.

"I'm solving a problem in me head."

"Isla?"

"Aye. Merry I believe I've been approaching this all the wrong way from the very beginning. We must stop playing this silly game of trying to make her jealous. I must find a way to get her to tell me what's wrong."

Merry smiled warmly at him. "I believe yer on the right track."

"Merry, how is it that yer always so cheerful?"

"Me Ma says 'tis because my name is Merry and I can hardly be any other way."

"Ye are a sweet and lovely lass. Why are ye nae married?"

"Nae one has asked," she replied. "Nae to say that I would marry the first one to ask. I'd like to fall in love with someone and then marry."

Aleck thought about what Merry had just said. Would he want Isla to marry him if she wasn't in love with him? Nay. It wouldn't be fair to either one of them. He was going to have to do his best to earn Isla's love, but more importantly, her trust. Without trust and respect for one another they didn't stand a chance.

"Merry, I think I know what I need to do."

CHAPTER 11

T HE FOLLOWING MORNING, Aleck awoke feeling much happier and more relaxed than he'd been since Isla's arrival. He had a plan and with that knowledge, he felt that no matter what happened with her, they would both be fine. He jogged down the stairs and out to the stables, where he ordered the lads to saddle his horse and Isla's. He then went to the kitchen and asked cook to pack him enough food for two and to deliver it to the stable boys.

Taegen approached him as he was about to enter the castle doors. "Sir, I wanted to apologize for not speaking with ye about the lass Isla practicing with me. If I had known that it was against yer wishes, I never would have encouraged her."

"She may practice with ye all she wishes, Taegen. Ye did the right thing. It was I who was wrong. 'Tis all settled now. The only thing I ask is that yer careful not to hurt her."

"I dinnae believe ye need to worry about that, sir. 'Tis I who may end up with an injury," he chuckled.

Aleck joined him. He'd mistakenly thought he was protecting her, when the only one she needed protecting from was himself and the crazy idea he held of how a lady should behave.

Taegen glanced at the horses. "Where are ye off to this morn?"

"I'm taking Isla for a ride across the property."

"Do ye wish me to join ye?"

"Nae. We'll be fine without your escort."

"As ye wish." Taegen bowed and walked away.

Aleck was about to enter the great hall to find Isla, but she was headed his way. He was feeling confident once again. His plan would succeed.

Isla broke her fast and decided she needed some fresh air. Merry wasn't feeling well and had stayed abed this morning, so she was on her own. She thought she'd go check on her horse and then perhaps go for a walk around the courtyard. It wasn't the most exciting of plans, but she preferred to be outdoors in the fresh air instead of stuck in the castle all day.

As she entered the courtyard and turned towards the stable, she was surprised to run into Aleck, who despite yesterday's events, seemed quite happy to see her.

"Isla, good day to ye. I've had our horses saddled. We're going to go for a morning ride."

She tamped down the urge she had to tell him that he couldn't simply order her to go for a ride with him and instead surprised herself by saying. "That would be lovely."

Apparently she wasn't the only one who was surprised. "You'd enjoy that?" he asked.

"I would," she responded with a smile on her face.

"Well, then, shall we?" She could see that he was about to offer her his arm, but thought better of it.

She surprised him again by taking it anyway. This war she'd been waging on Laird Sinclair was only serving to make them both miserable. Hopefully, a ride through the countryside would set them on a new path.

Once they were mounted, Aleck asked, "Ye willnae be afraid to be alone with me?" He sounded a bit unsure of himself and Isla reminded herself that her behavior had affected him more than she thought possible.

"Nae. Of course not." She adjusted herself in the saddle and then followed Aleck out through the gates.

"Come ride by my side, Isla." He slowed his horse so she could catch up with him.

She had to admit to herself that she felt a bit uncomfortable with this situation and hoped she hadn't made a mistake by joining him. "How far are we going?" she asked.

"Nae too far." He smiled warmly at her. "I'd like to show you why I love this land so much."

She returned his smile and relaxed. This was going to be fine, as long as she did her best to be pleasant.

Aleck took the opportunity to point out certain landmarks to her and she found she was interested.

"When I was but a lad, I would ride out this way often. I believed I was a warrior and would search behind the trees and rocks for enemies who werenae there." He laughed at the thought of it.

"Ye had a good imagination," she commented.

"Aye. I believed in the elves and the faeries and all manner of creatures."

"Believed?" she asked.

"I still believe."

Isla tipped her head and gazed at him, perhaps seeing him for the first time as something more than the laird of the castle.

"Were ye a happy lad?"

"For the most part." Aleck told her about growing up here, racing horses with his friends. Isla pictured him as a young lad riding like the devil himself was after him across the fields and along the craggy hilltops. "Will and I had a favorite tree." He pointed to a large oak up ahead. "That one there. We'd spend an entire day up in its branches pretending to be highwaymen."

Isla laughed at this. "I cannae picture ye pretending to be a bad man."

"We never robbed anyone," he assured her with a chuckle. "It was all in our imaginations, ye see."

She liked this side of Aleck. She wanted to know more. "What other things did ye do?"

"We wished to be knights, ye ken. We'd gather other lads from the village and we'd have our own tournaments. Find tree branches to use as jousting poles."

The look of sheer joy on his face as he spoke warmed Isla's heart. "It seems yer childhood was filled with much fun and friends."

"Aye. There were times when there was sadness," he answered, the joy of only a moment ago leaving his handsome face.

"Ye speak of yer sister."

"That was a cloud that hung over our family beyond the passing of me Ma and Da. They missed her terribly, as did I. I ken that I didnae even know her, but the way they spoke of her brought her to life."

"'Tis good she's back."

Aleck nodded. "We're almost there. It is just across the stream and up the other side of the hill."

Her heart almost stopped. Isla had been so caught up in his stories that she didn't hear the stream. But now she could. The water rushed over rocks in the stream, making small swirling eddies near the banks.

She wouldn't let him know she feared the water. She refused to ask him for help. Instead she focused on controlling her breathing, sat up straighter and wore an aura of fearlessness.

As they approached the banks of the stream, Isla reined her horse to a stop. She drew in a deep breath to quell the uneasiness she was feeling.

Aleck continued on unaware of the terror she felt when near the water. His horse began to wade into the stream. "We're going to cross to the other side. There's a beautiful view of the valley and we should be able to see clear to Ben Nevis."

She watched as his horse continued to the middle of the stream. The water crept up with every step until Aleck was wet to his knees. Panic seized her. She couldn't move.

The horse continued forward to the other side and out on to the shore. He shook a bit and drops flew onto the flowers that lined the bank. "Are ye coming?" he asked.

She wanted to say no, but her pride wouldn't allow her to appear like a fragile, frightened woman in his presence. She urged her horse forward. Lily had never crossed a stream before because Isla had never asked her to. She must have felt Isla's trepidation because the horse stopped at the water's edge and backed away.

"Do ye need my help?" Aleck asked.

No, Isla thought. She would do this alone. She would never need his help. With a soft kick to the flank, she urged her horse forward once again. This time she went, tentatively at first and then at a quicker pace right into the middle of the stream where she stopped and stuck her nose into the rushing water, then pulling her nose up and out she sent a splash across the rushing surface of the water. She seemed to think this was fun as she continued to splash with her nose and her hooves. With the water almost past her ankles, the movement was causing large drops to splash onto Isla's arms and face. Isla was frozen in the saddle. Her horse wasn't interested in continuing through the stream. Aleck, oblivious to her fear, sat on the other bank laughing at her predicament. This only served to anger Isla, who suddenly pulled back on the reins in an attempt to get Lily to stop playing. The horse reared up in response and Isla promptly fell from her back into the icy water. She gasped for breath as she flailed around helplessly. Lily bolted from the water, leaving her behind.

She felt herself being dragged downstream, all the while clawing at the water to keep her head from going under. Out of nowhere, two strong arms gathered her up and out of the water. Without thinking she clung to her rescuer, shivering and shaking.

"'Tis alright, lass. I've got ye now." Aleck spoke softly and calmly as he walked back to the shore. "Dinnae fear. Ye've nae drowned." He sat down on the banks of the stream, with Isla in his lap.

Isla clung to him, unable to let go. "I cannae swim."

"I thought as much," he said. He continued rubbing her back. Each comforting stroke brought her breathing closer to normal. "Yer horse seemed to enjoy herself."

"She's never been in the water before," Isla explained. He laughed a bit at that and she could feel the warmth swirl around her.

"Why did ye nae tell me? I wouldnae have left ye on yer own to cross."

Isla studied his jawline, and tucked her head into his neck. "I didnae wish ye to believe I was afraid," she admitted in a tiny voice.

"I wouldnae have thought any less of ye, lass. We all have fears."

"Even ye?"

"Even me."

"What are ye afraid of?" she asked of his chin.

"I dinnae like spiders," Aleck said.

She looked up at that, "But they're so small." She felt the hint of a smile in the corner of her mouth.

"It doesnae matter how big or small. When I see one 'tis all I can do to nae scream like a bairn."

Isla laughed at the picture that created in her mind. Aleck laughed along with her and just like that, the last of her panic was gone.

"Yer lips have turned blue. Here. Let me stand up." Aleck moved her from his lap and Isla became acutely aware of just how cold she was. She watched as he walked to his horse and pulled a plaid from his saddle bag. He handed it to her. "Ye should get out of that dress." Aleck suggested. His voice seemed to catch on the words, and he coughed a bit. "I'll turn me back so that ye can disrobe and wrap yerself up. I'll be right here."

Isla reluctantly did as she was told. Hiding behind some nearby shrubs she shed her clothing and wrapped herself completely in the plaid.

"Ye can look now," she said.

Aleck turned and faced her. "Come here." He motioned for her to join him and he took her clothes from her hands, laying them out in the sun to dry. He then ran his hands up and down her arms and her back, warming her all the way to her core. The strange sensation she was feeling was one she hadn't experienced since Derrick's passing. She wanted to stop him, but somehow couldn't bring herself to do it. When he was done, he held her close in his arms and she let him. She could go back to her old defensive ways once she was safe and warm, she told herself. She glanced up and was surprised to see his eyes focused on hers. The look in them was one she wasn't prepared for. She tried to look away, but it seemed he'd cast some spell upon her and she was unable to. She wanted to speak, but the words wouldn't come. His face, his lips were so close she could feel his warm breath upon her face.

"Isla," he whispered.

She closed her eyes. She knew what he was thinking and feeling and she felt herself giving in to those strong yearnings that had lain dormant for so long. His hand stroked her cheek, brushing wet locks of hair aside. Would this ever stop? Did she want it to? In truth, no. She wanted to feel his lips on hers and as if he read her mind, she felt the soft warmth of them as they gently brushed hers. His hands cupped her face and he kissed her again, this time deeply and with passion. She gave in to the warmth of his kiss, her body melting against his felt so right.

But it wasn't right. It was very, very wrong. She pushed at him with the palms of her hands. "Please, stop. I cannae."

He let her go. "I'm sorry, Isla. I shouldnae have done it, but I couldnae help myself."

Isla pulled the plaid tight around herself, at once missing his embrace and needing the distance from him to think straight. "Nae need to apologize. I dinnae regret it, but it cannae happen ever again."

ALECK FELT AS if he'd been slapped. Her words stung. She'd enjoyed that. He knew she had. He felt her body leaning into his as she most heartily returned his kisses.

"Will ye tell me why?" he asked.

Isla looked to the sky for answers, then the trees, but didn't seem to find them. "I cannae explain it to ye or to anyone." He could feel her putting up the wall of her defenses again.

"What has happened to ye, Isla? What has made ye believe that love isnae fer ye?" It tore at his heart to think of what could possibly have caused her to shut herself off to the happiness that love would bring.

She avoided his question. "How will we get back to the castle? I cannae go in the stream again."

Aleck understood that he wouldn't be getting anymore information from Isla this day. He'd made progress with her. More than he'd imagined possible at the beginning of their ride. Somehow he had to find out what was holding her back. Once he did, he was sure he could convince her to let him love her, but for now he would be happy with the sweetest kiss he'd ever enjoyed.

"Ye can ride with me." He closed the distance between them. He desperately wanted to hold her again, to make her forget the pain she had been through. But he didn't touch her, he just stared into those beautiful eyes. "I'll hold ye safe and willnae allow ye to come to any harm. Do ye trust me, Isla?" This was a question he wasn't sure she would answer.

And she didn't. "My clothes arenae dry."

"Dinnae fash about yer clothes. I know a more private way into the castle. Nary a soul will see ye."

He could see her mind working as she decided whether or not to go along with his plan.

"Ye promise ye willnae let me fall?"

"I promise."

She nodded her head and walked to Brychan. Aleck picked up her clothing and affixed it to her horse.

"There. I dinnae believe they'll fall off." He then easily lifted Isla in his strong arms, and placed her atop his horse. He tied Lily's reins to his saddle and then vaulted up behind Isla. Placing his arms around her and grasping his reins he spoke to his steed. "Walk on, Brychan."

Isla gripped his forearm with her hands and buried her face in his chest as he easily navigated the water, getting them to the other side without incident.

"Ye asked me earlier if I trust ye." Isla didn't move her head from his chest, but she did loosen her grasp on his arm.

"And do ye?"

"Aye."

Aleck's heart filled with the joy of that simple statement. She trusted him. "I promise ye, Isla. I'll never do anything to betray that trust."

CHAPTER 12

EDINBURGH 2017

D YLAN PLACED HIS laptop on the table at the bakery. Maureen and her husband David looked over his shoulder as he navigated his way to his family tree.

"There. You see. We are related. We're cousins a few times removed, but cousins nonetheless."

"Amazing," Maureen said. "What a small world we live in that ye'd find yer way to this little bakery."

"We should have dinner together later today. What do you say? Our treat." Dylan hoped they'd say yes. It would help to further their agenda with regard to Molly.

"I dinnae think we can. We've wee Molly to think of," Maureen said. Her hands clenched in her lap, and Dylan had the sense that her concern was not just about bringing a toddler to a restaurant.

"Bring her along." Dylan glanced over at Molly, who was happily seated in a high chair at the table playing with Maggie's keys.

"Oh, I dunno. What do ye think, David?"

David placed a comforting arm around Maureen, "I'd love to have dinner with me cousin and if he doesnae mind Molly joining us, I think we should say yes."

Maureen nodded, "Alright, then. We'll go."

"Great. We'll be back later to get ye," Maggie said. "And now, little lady, if ye dinnae mind. I'll need me keys back." She held her hand out and Molly plunked the keys into her palm. "Thank ye."

Maureen distracted Molly with a set of wooden spoons from the kitchen of the bakery. Dylan and Maggie waved goodbye and left them.

"THAT WENT WELL," Dylan said.

"Why wouldn't it?" Maggie asked.

"Oh, I don't know. Despite the fact we're related, we're perfect strangers to them. The real difficulty will be when we try to convince them to let Anania have Molly."

"We have to try. Perhaps the perfect moment will present itself tonight."

"I hope so. If I were them, I'd be pretty skeptical about this whole thing."

"What do ye say we do a little sightseeing?" Maggie asked.

Dylan eagerly agreed. "Where should we go first?"

"Let's go to the castle, I've been wanting to see it for a verra long time."

"I can't believe you've lived in Scotland your whole life and you've never made it to Edinburgh."

"Crazy, I know, but true." Maggie wrapped an arm around his waist and kissed his cheek.

"Let's drop my laptop off in the room." Dylan's sensual smile elicited a knowing look from his wife.

"We're just dropping off the laptop, right?"

Dylan pitched his voice lower, "Of course. What else would we be doing?"

She wrinkled her nose and rolled her eyes. "We've got lots to see and this might be our last chance before things start happening."

"I know, babe." He kissed her nose. "Maybe later?"

"Definitely later," Maggie laughed.

"HOW'S EVERYTHING GOING?" Edna asked.

"Fine." said Maggie. "We're having dinner with Maureen and David tonight. They're bringing Molly along. I can't talk too much longer, I've got to finish getting ready."

"So, they know they're related to Dylan now, do they?"

"Aye. We showed them his family tree. They were delighted."

"Good. Keep a close watch on Molly. I've been getting reports from Anania and she fears that this man is getting closer and closer to stealing her away."

"We will. I feel like her mother and father are aware of something already, but they havenae said a thing. Maybe tonight they'll talk to us about it."

"I hope so. 'Twould make your job much easier if they understood the gravity of the situation."

"One way or another, they will."

"I'll let ye go, love. Be careful."

"Bye, Auntie."

Maggie hung up the phone and finished getting dressed. Dylan was ready and waiting for her, seated on the bed and watching television. "Okay. Let's go." She grabbed her purse and Dylan turned off the TV.

The elevator doors opened almost as soon as they pressed the button. They entered and found they weren't alone. Several others were heading down to the lobby and the elevator was so full they barely fit. Maggie elbowed Dylan, whispering, "Something doesnae feel right."

He didn't say a thing. As they disembarked the elevator, Dylan glanced around at the other passengers, as did Maggie.

"Is it the same man?" he asked.

"I'm nae sure. It was hard to pinpoint considering how many were in the elevator."

"Okay. We'll need to keep our eyes open."

"Right."

They walked across the street, and into the stairwell entrance beside the bakery. Maureen and David were already downstairs getting little Molly settled into the pram.

"Any suggestions on where we should eat?" Dylan asked.

"There's a nice little place right down the street. Good food and they have highchairs for Molly."

"Let's go. I'm verra hungry," Maggie said.

David and Dylan walked in the lead and Maggie walked behind with Maureen and Molly. "How old is Molly?" Maggie asked.

"She's eighteen months."

"So she walks pretty well then?"

"Aye," Maureen seemed distracted and kept turning to look behind them.

"Is everything alright?"

"I dinnae ken. I keep feeling like someone is following us."

"Really?"

"Every time I go out with Molly I get the same feeling."

"Hmmm…" Maggie looked behind as well. She knew why Maureen was having this feeling. She was having it as well. Whoever was after Molly was right behind them, but he was doing a good job of remaining in the shadows. She wished he'd show himself.

"Sometimes I feel like I'm just being a paranoid new Mum, ye ken?"

"Since I have nae children yet, I can't say I do, but I believe in intuition and in feelings. 'Tis always best to be careful."

"I'm happy ye don't think me daft," Maureen said.

"Of course not. I'll let ye in on a little secret." Maggie was about to spill the beans. She hoped she wasn't making a mistake. It wouldn't take much to spook Maureen and David, but Maureen was already spooked. She had to let her know that what she was feeling was real evil and not just paranoia. It was imperative that Maureen and David know she was there to help them and to keep them all safe.

"What's that?"

"I'm a witch. So's me Aunt Edna." There she'd said it. She waited on pins and needles for Maureen's response.

"A real witch?" Maureen seemed surprised by this. She stopped and turned to Maggie, examining her from head to toe with a bemused expression.

"We dinnae wear pointy hats or dress all in black, but aye, we're real witches." Maggie held her breath, waiting for an outburst or some other outward sign that Maureen didn't believe her.

"My goodness, I would never have guessed." She turned back and started walking once again.

"So, if ye need any help, ye can count on me." Maggie emphasized, "I'm a good witch, ye ken?"

"Can ye feel what I'm feeling then?" Maureen asked.

Maggie was thankful that she seemed curious rather than dismissive. "Aye. I can."

Maureen stiffened, her face turning ashen, her eyes blinking rapidly. "Then I really do have something to worry about." Despite the outward signs that she was afraid, Maureen's voice was light and smooth.

"I'm afraid so. Dylan and I will speak with ye once we get to the restaurant." Maggie took hold of Maureen's arm to keep her from stumbling. She seemed a bit unsteady on her feet. "Are ye alright?"

"Aye. I will be." Maureen's voice came out in a whisper.

They walked the rest of the way in silence and Maggie worried that she'd said too much, too soon. The cat was out of the bag now, so there wasn't much she could do but hope they were receptive to what they were about to hear.

PIERCE WALKED IN the shadows on the other side of the street. He was going to need to make his move soon. He wondered who these other two people were. He'd seen them in the elevator of his hotel and now they were walking down the street with the Sinclairs. They must be going to dinner, he thought. Maureen Sinclair kept peering around behind her. She was obviously aware of his presence. He didn't quite understand how, but nonetheless it wouldn't prevent him from kidnapping Molly.

They entered a small restaurant called Tartan Jack's and after waiting about ten minutes, he went in as well.

"How many, sir?"

"One."

"This way, please." Pierce followed the hostess as she led him to a small table in the back of the restaurant where he had a perfect view of the Sinclair family. They were all chatting away happily. Molly was seated in a highchair closer to the center of the restaurant and in direct line with the door. His hope was that they would be so engrossed in conversation that he could sweep Molly up out of the high chair and make a run for it. He'd studied the area and he knew all the little backstreets and alleys like the back of his hands. In the meantime, he may as well eat. If things went well, he wasn't sure when he'd have another decent meal.

MAGGIE WAS AWARE of the exact moment the mystery man entered the restaurant. He was seated in the back and he'd been watching them closely as they ate. She was seated in such a position that she had a clear view of him. He was not quite as tall as Dylan and he wore his hair closely cropped. He looked like a business man on holiday, but she knew that wasn't the case. She could feel his malevolent intent emanating across the restaurant. Now was as good a time as any to start this conversation about Molly.

"Maureen, ye were telling me that ye've had a bad feeling that someone is watching ye, right?"

"Aye. I can still feel it here in the restaurant. Lately I dinnae wish to go out. I'm afraid of what might happen."

"I think she's suffering from post-partum anxiety," David added.

"Molly is a year and a half, David. Surely 'tis too late for that," Maureen said.

"What she's feeling is quite real," Maggie said. All eyes turned to her. Maggie took a deep breath, knowing they had crossed the point of no return. They were going to tell the Sinclairs about the threat to their family and they would either accept Maggie and Dylan's help, or run screaming in the other direction.

Maureen lowered her voice and turned towards David. "Maggie's told me she's a witch and she felt the same thing as we walked down the street."

"A witch?" David chuckled nervously at this.

"It's true," Dylan assured him. David turned to him, then to Maggie and back to Dylan, searching their faces for the joke.

"I haven't just felt it tonight. I've felt evil in my hotel and now here in the restaurant."

"Are they here? The person who's been following me?" Maureen glanced frantically around the room.

"Aye. He is. We must act as if nothing's wrong, ye ken?"

They all glanced at Molly who was happily playing with her food. The adults, on the other hand, had forgotten their food.

"I'm sorry." Maggie said, "I didn't mean to ruin our meal, but Dylan and I have come to Edinburgh with a message for ye from me Aunt Edna and from the Elven Queen Anania."

"Did ye say Elven Queen?" David wore an expression of disbelief.

Maureen elbowed him. "Go on, please."

"There's a man who wishes to take Molly away. He believes she is the key to wealth and power."

"Me Molly?" Maureen placed a hand on her chest and the other over her mouth.

"He believes it to be yer Molly. His plan, according to Anania, is to kidnap her and take her back in time. I'm nae sure why he needs her, but he ultimately wants something called the Twin Sword. Legend says that whoever has it will have unlimited powers and wealth."

"This all sounds incredible. I cannae believe it." David was shaking his head.

"What can we do? Should we call the police?" Maureen asked.

"They probably wouldn't believe you," Dylan said.

"I know this is difficult to hear, but the man is quite intent on taking Molly. Aunt Edna and Anania would like you to give Molly to them. They'll keep her safe until we can deal with this man."

Maureen looked horrified, "No. I can't be away from Molly. I won't do it." Her voice was rising and Maggie knew she needed to regain control of the discussion.

"Ye'd have nae need to worry about her. She'd be well cared for and hopefully back with you in no time." Maggie kept her voice quiet and reassuring. This was not going well at all.

"This is crazy. Are ye really my cousin? Or did ye just come here to take our child away from us?" David's demeanor changed drastically from earlier. He went from being thrilled about meeting a new cousin to enraged. Sweat broke out on his forehead, his nostrils flared and his face turned a frightening shade of red. He was shouting now and others in the restaurant were taking note.

"I really am your cousin, David. This person needs Molly because she's a Sinclair." Dylan did his best to keep his voice calm as he spoke.

Maggie reached out to touch David's arm, but he brushed it aside, abruptly standing. "Thank ye much for dinner. Maureen, we're leaving. He picked Molly up from the highchair and marched out the door with Maureen trailing behind him.

CHAPTER 13

"Now what?" Dylan asked, glancing around the restaurant, which had come to a complete standstill as staff and diners all seemed to be staring at them. He looked back at Maggie unsure of what to do next.

"That didn't go the way I planned," Maggie said, feeling shell-shocked by what had just taken place.

"It couldn't have gone worse," Dylan said. "What would you suggest our next move should be?"

"I don't know. I guess we hang around and wait for him to make his move."

In all the commotion, Dylan forgot that the man they were after had been sitting at the back of the restaurant and he'd seen and heard everything. He glanced back at the table where the man was seated and he was gone. "He's gone, Maggie!"

"Oh, no!" she shouted, jumping up from her seat.

Dylan was on his feet as well. "We should get outside and make sure the Sinclairs are okay."

They hurriedly called their waitress over and handed her more than enough money to cover the bill and the tip, before rushing out the door and back towards the bakery.

The sound of a scream pierced the night. Dylan and Maggie immediately bolted down the street towards the sounds of Maureen sobbing.

"Where are David and Molly?" Dylan asked.

Maureen pointed down a darkened alley way.

"You stay here with Maureen. I'll go after them." Dylan ran down the alleyway, leaving the two women behind. In the dim light, he could barely make out someone running up ahead. "David!" he called.

No answer. He continued running, but the figure up ahead had stopped. David was doubled over, out of breath. "I can't see them anymore. I don't know where they are."

"Catch your breath. I'll go after them." Dylan continued on down the alleyway. It opened out onto a well lit street bordered by a park. He looked in all directions, but his gut was telling him the park was where he should go.

He took off at a sprint until he reached the edge of the park. There was someone up ahead of him moving quickly. The man turned and Dylan caught a glimpse of the bundle in his arms. Molly. It had to be her. He slowed down and cautiously approached, taking cover behind trees intermittently set along the pathway. He was almost there when he saw a greenish pinpoint of light begin to emerge, getting larger and larger until it lit the entire area. A woman appeared and grabbed Molly from the stunned man. She disappeared back into the light, taking Molly with her. Dylan couldn't believe his eyes. The light faded and everything was black until his eyes could adjust to the dark night again. Molly was gone and when he focused back to where the man had been, so was he. Had he followed Anania and Molly or had he run off? Dylan jogged further into the park, his senses on high alert. They were gone. It was as if they'd never been in the park at all. He turned back to find David standing in the exact spot where little Molly had disappeared.

"She's gone," he said, his voice quiet and unsure.

"I'm sorry. I tried to get to them, but I was too late." Dylan was completely out of breath. He bent forward, hands on knees for a moment to catch his breath.

"I saw it. I saw the woman take Molly." David's panic was becoming evident. He whipped his head around, obviously searching the dark park for his daughter. He stopped, breathing hard and raking his hands through his hair in frustration.

"Did you see where that guy went?" Dylan straightened and

glanced around. It was too dark to see much of anything.

"No. I didn't." David was obviously in shock. "Oh, my God! What am I going to tell Maureen?" he sobbed. "I couldn't save her. I couldn't protect her."

Dylan placed a hand on David's back. He hoped to ease his mind. "If Anania took Molly, it is only to protect her. To keep her from harm."

"I don't believe that!" David glanced suspiciously at Dylan, shaking his hand off of his back.

There was nothing Dylan could do or say to console David, whose face was buried in his hands as loud sobs wracked his body. He felt responsible. If things had gone differently at the restaurant, Molly would still be with them.

MAUREEN BEGAN TO cry when she saw David and Dylan coming back down the alley. "Where's Molly?" Where is she?"

"Anania took her," Dylan said.

"What? How?" Maggie was relieved it was Anania who had Molly, but her heart was breaking for Maureen and David. She could only imagine how devastated they must feel.

Maureen was crying so much that she was unable to speak. She went to her husband, who wrapped his arms around her and tucked his face into her neck.

"She appeared out of nowhere. A green light brought her and she grabbed Molly away from the guy and disappeared."

"Did ye catch him?" Maggie asked Dylan. She realized that was a silly question. If he had, wouldn't he be with them now.

"He disappeared as well. I don't know if he went with Anania or if he ran off. I tried to find him, but couldn't." Dylan lowered his head and then gazed up at her with sadness in his eyes.

"We should call the police." David straightened his shoulders.

His voice was once again strong and determined.

"What are we going to tell them? They'd never believe our story," Dylan responded.

"Come, let's go back to yer apartment. We'll contact me Aunt Edna. She'll do her best to explain things to ye." Her aunt had put her faith in her and she would be disappointed to hear that Maggie failed. Maggie was angry with herself. She should have known better than to try to explain things to the Sinclairs in a public place when they had obviously been followed by this mad man. She mentally berated herself, but knew that there wasn't time for self-pity. She needed to speak with Edna. She'd know exactly how to handle things.

Maureen was sobbing uncontrollably now and David looked to be doing his best not to join her. He placed an arm around her shoulders and guided the now empty stroller back down the street to the bakery. They entered through the side door and headed upstairs.

"What's wrong?" they ran into Mrs. May on the stairs. No one answered and she followed them into the apartment. "Maureen, where's wee Molly?"

Maureen was unable to speak, overcome by more wracking sobs. She picked up a stuffed bear from the floor and hugged it to herself. She walked to the front window and looked out.

"Oh, no! What's happened?" Mrs. May appeared frantic. She looked first to Molly, then David and when neither one of them answered, she turned to Maggie and Dylan.

"Please, sit, Mrs. May. Maureen, ye should sit as well," Maggie said. She took Maureen by the arm and guided her to the large overstuffed chair next to the fireplace. Seeing a box of tissues on an end table, she grabbed it and set it in Maureen's lap.

Maggie waved her hand in front of the small fireplace occupying a spot in the living room and a fire blazed to life. Mrs. May practically jumped out of her chair and appeared quite frightened by what she was seeing. Her eyes darted back and forth between Maggie and the fire. David, who was sitting on the arm of Maureen's chair when the fire popped and sparked in the hearth, protectively shielded Maureen from it, as he looked on in disbelief. "Auntie? 'Tis me. Are ye there?"

The fire crackled and popped and everyone but Dylan sat with their mouths agape. Mrs. May seemed to wish she could disappear into the sofa.

"I'm here, Maggie." Edna's voice rang throught he room, loud and clear, causing another round of shock and disbelief.

"Auntie, I believe Anania has taken Molly," Maggie said. She glanced around the room and as she'd expected, the Sinclairs and Mrs. May seemed stupefied by what they were seeing and hearing.

"I saw it all, my dear," Edna responded. "Maureen, dinnae fash. We'll get Molly back to ye as soon as possible. She is safe." This seemed to settle Maureen. She sat up straighter and her tears stopped.

"Wh-wh-where is she?" she stammered.

"She's with David's many times great grandfather in the year 1517 at Sinclair castle. Aleck Sinclair will guard her and keep her from harm until 'tis safe to bring her home."

Maggie understood that the mere sound of Edna's voice was beginning to work its magic on David, Maureen and Mrs. May.

"Are ye saying she's time travelled?" David asked. He was now standing and speaking into the fireplace.

"She has. Now, we must find this man, whoever he is and keep him from getting to her," Edna said.

"He disappeared," Dylan said. "We don't know if he's in this time or in the past."

"Anania will be in touch with me and I'll find out where he is. Dinnae fear. I've got this all under control. It will all be taken care of," she assured them.

"We dinnae know ye at all. Why should we believe ye?" David asked.

"I dinnae believe ye've any other choice."

CHAPTER 14

A LECK STOOD OUTSIDE the door to Isla's bed chamber. He was there to make sure she was feeling better after the events of the previous day. However, he found himself eavesdropping, which he knew was wrong, but he couldn't help himself.

"I nearly drowned, Merry!" Isla exclaimed.

"But ye didnae. Aleck saved ye," Merry answered.

Aleck was proud of himself. He *had* saved Isla and because he did, he got to enjoy the feel of her in his arms for more than just a moment or two.

"He did and it is all your fault! You told him I was afraid of water, didn't ye?" Isla's voice was raised in anger.

"Why would ye think that? I cannae believe that ye would accuse me of such a thing," Merry answered.

"'Tis only that ye keep trying to throw me together with Aleck when ye ken that I dinnae wish it."

Aleck couldn't see them, but he could hear Isla stomping around the room. He assumed it was Isla, because he couldn't imagine that Merry ever stomped.

"Why are ye so difficult, Isla?" Merry kept her tone reasonable.

"Because 'tis ye he should marry, nae me," Isla snarled.

Aleck was a bit taken aback by this.

"I dinnae wish to marry him," Merry yelled, her reasonable tone gone. "I've told ye before and I'm telling ye again. I have nae wish to be Lady Sinclair. 'Tis ye who should marry him."

"I dinnae wish to marry him either," Isla said. "I'm quite sure ye've heard me say that many times."

"So, why are ye both here?" Aleck pushed the door open and entered the room, much to the surprise and embarrassment of both sisters. "If I didnae know better, I'd believe that I was the most undesirable of men. I believe me feelings have been hurt." He didn't have to try very hard to appear wounded by their conversation.

The sisters both appeared to be remorseful for what they'd said. Their faces were red with shame as they squirmed and fidgeted under his scrutiny. "We're sorry," Merry said. "We didnae ken ye were standing there."

"Ye would have said it no matter," Aleck said. He wondered how he found himself in this predicament. Two sisters. Both of marriageable age and neither of them wanted anything to do with him. He'd speak with Nick about this crazy idea he'd hatched for him to marry his sister, but in the meantime they were here at his castle and he'd do his best to be a good host. "I don't imagine ye'd care to go riding with me? I promise we willnae go near any water." He gazed pointedly at Isla. He thought that both sisters would feel sufficiently guilty that they'd go for the ride whether they wanted to or not.

The two sisters exchanged glances and then Isla said, "Of course we'd be happy to join ye."

Merry nodded in agreement.

"Good. I've got the horses waiting outside fer us. Shall we?"

Aleck led the way and looked back to be sure they were following him. They were. He was quite sure he'd noticed Merry who wore a huge grin, winking at him. He wasn't sure what she was up to, but he knew he'd find out soon enough.

Outside, Aleck gave Isla a leg up onto her horse, surprised that she accepted his help, and turned to help Merry, but before he could get to her she stopped him.

"I'm afraid I cannae join ye. I forgot that I was planning to work with cook today. We're finishing up the menu for Kat's feast."

"Merry!" Isla said.

"I'm sorry! I really did forget. Go on without me, please. I dinnae wish to ruin yer day."

Isla's eyes narrowed as she gazed on her sister with suspicion. Nevertheless, she made no move to dismount.

Aleck mounted his own horse. "Alright then. We willnae be long."

They pointed the horses towards the gates and walked through, heading in the opposite direction from the stream. Aleck noted Isla seemed nervous.

"I promise there is nae water involved in today's ride." He was still feeling hurt by what he'd heard and knowing that Isla would probably rather be anywhere other than with him wasn't helping.

"I believe ye," she replied.

"Good."

They rode on in silence until they came to a spot that afforded them a view of the valley beneath. They stopped and looked out over it.

"'Tis beautiful," Isla said, her voice soft and reverent.

"'Tis one of me favorite places. I come here often to sit and think." He glanced over and was pleased to see Isla smiling at him.

"I can see it would be a good place to do just that," she said.

"Isla, I wonder if I might ask you about something, and I wonder if you'll answer me honestly." Aleck wasn't sure this was going to go well, but despite the fact that he now completely understood that Isla wished to have nothing to do with him, he wanted to help her. She was obviously burdened by something and as her friend, as someone who cared deeply for her, he wanted to help and he hoped she'd let him.

"Ye may ask, but I'm nay sure what ye wish to ken and so I cannae say whether I will answer at all."

She was being honest with him. He thought for a moment. He wanted to be careful here. "Why do ye nae wish to marry?"

She was quiet for some time and he imagined she didnae wish to say. He was about to speak again when she surprised him. "I will answer yer question and I will be honest. I've kept this secret close to me heart for quite some time, but 'tis nae fair to leave ye wondering why I cannae marry."

"Cannae or willnae?"

"Either way the answer would be the same." She turned in her saddle to face him. "Aleck, ye are a good man and a handsome one. I'd be lying to us both if I said I didnae feel something fer ye."

"Well, 'tis a start." A spark of hope lit in his heart, but was quickly extinguished.

"Nae. It must be a finish. Ye see, I had a fiancé not so verra long ago. His name was Derrick." She looked down at her hands as she adjusted her reins.

He was surprised to hear this, but did his best to hide it. "Did he break yer heart?"

"In a way, but not the way ye imagine. He was one of the finest Mackall warriors. Tall, strong, handsome. I loved him more than life itself. One day as he was riding home from a neighboring castle, he was set upon by five riders. He bravely battled them, but five against one are nae good odds." Isla sat up taller in her saddle and gazed out over the valley below.

"Was he killed?" Aleck felt her pain, even as she tried to keep it buried inside.

"He was gravely wounded. They left him for dead, but me Derrick was able to mount his horse and head back to Dunnet Head. As his horse came through the gate, I ran to him. I could see he was badly wounded and I called for help. He slid from his horse and to the ground. As I held his head in me lap, he told me what had happened. He was so weak. He'd lost so much blood." She became choked up at this point, unable to speak.

Aleck didnae say a word. He waited for her to regain her composure.

"With his last breath he told me that he loved me and that there had never been another for him. Before I could answer him, he was gone. I vowed that as I was the only one for him, there would never be another for me. I could never love another, so ye can see

95

why I cannae marry." She didn't look his way, instead keeping her gaze steadily ahead.

Aleck wanted more than anything to reach out and pluck Isla from her horse. He wanted to hold her in his arms and comfort her. He now understood her hurt and her anger. "I dinnae ken the words that will comfort ye. I'm so verra sorry."

"Thank ye. I'm sorry that I cannae marry ye. Ye'd be a good husband I'm sure." She turned to him, a sad smile on her lips.

Her words were no consolation. He had dreamed of a life with her, but now realized there would be none. It saddened him. He couldn't imagine that Derrick would want Isla to live a solitary life in his memory, but he wasn't about to say that to her. Not here. Not now. She was still grieving his loss.

Silently they made their way along the edge of the overlook and then back into open fields. A storm was approaching and would be upon them in no time. The wind had picked up and along with it came dark, ominous clouds that promised a downpour at any moment. Aleck rode close to Isla and wrapped a plaid around her shoulders. "We should head back."

They solemnly rode towards home, each of them lost in their own thoughts. Lightning flashed through the sky and with it came a loud rumble of thunder and the first drops of rain. They moved their horses up to a trot and continued on.

"What's that?" Isla asked, pointing to something moving in the grass up ahead.

"I cannae tell," Aleck answered.

They continued riding towards the moving object when the sounds of whimpering reached their ears. They both realized at the same time that what they were seeing was a small child seated within the tall grass. Aleck kicked his horse into a gallop and reached the bairn in seconds. Isla was close on his heels. He leapt from his saddle to find a wee lass holding her arms up to him while tears streamed down her cheeks. He picked her up and cradled her in his arms, wrapping her in his cloak. She quieted in his arms and he breathed a sigh of relief. He turned to Isla.

"A bairn!" she cried. "How did she get here?" She glanced around, as did Aleck. There was no one in sight.

"I'm nae sure. Why would someone leave a wee one here with a storm approaching?" He was baffled by it. The child gazed up at him and a sweet smile lit her face. "Dinnae fash wee one. Ye're safe. I willnae allow any harm to come to ye."

He walked to Isla. "Can ye ride with her in yer arms?"

She hesitated. "I'm nae good with wee ones."

Aleck cocked his head to the side, raising an eyebrow in disbelief. "Have ye nay held a bairn?"

She shook her head.

Aleck looked at the bairn and decided she was too big to simply wrap in his cloak. "I cannae mount while holding her. Ye'll have to take her until I am atop me horse." He handed the wee one to Isla, who held her as if she were a fragile object that might break in her arms. He strode the few feet to collect his horse and when he looked back he saw that the bairn had wrapped her arms around Isla's neck. Once astride, he maneuvered his horse closer and reached out for the bairn, but Isla held fast. "I'll keep her," she said. She'd tucked the wee one close to her chest and was staring into her eyes, brushing away her tears and cooing soft words to calm her.

"Are ye sure? I dinnae mind riding with her." He noted that whatever discomfort she had at first was now completely gone and had been replaced with wonder.

"She's a beauty," Isla said, clearly fascinated with her new charge.

"Aye. We must find out why she was left here. I'd search the area, but this storm grows stronger and we must get back before we are all soaked to the bone. 'Twould nae be good for the bairn." He reached over and repositioned the plaid to cover both Isla and the bairn.

"We should give her a name," Isla said, eyes fixed on the lass.

"She has a name, we just dinnae ken it."

"I know." Isla finally looked away from the little girl, but only to roll her eyes at him. "We cannae keep calling her 'the bairn'."

"Ye can think on it. Fer now we must get back."

They both took their horses to a canter. Aleck turned back to make sure Isla was alright and she seemed to have everything under control. By now the wind was howling and the sky was black. The rain drops were coming down in sheets. Once through the gates of the castle, Aleck jumped down from Brychan and ran to Isla who handed the bairn into his care. He waited for her to dismount and then they ran for the castle, entering the great hall and going straight to the hearth to warm themselves.

"Oh, good yer back," Merry entered the hall. "I was worried ye'd be caught in the storm." Her eyes immediately went to the child. "Who have we here?" Merry's voice, which was normally quite pleasant to hear, took on a new sing-song quality as she spoke to the bairn. Aleck smiled, of course Merry would take to the child.

"We found her," Isla said. "She was sitting all alone in the field." Her voice, normally a bit sharper than Merry's even when she was in a good mood, had changed to that same sing-song sweetness. Aleck's smile grew a little bigger. It seemed Isla's heart was not so closed off as she thought.

"A changeling?" Merry asked.

"Nae. I dinnae believe it," Isla said.

"Nor do I," Aleck added.

"But what other explanation can there be for her presence in the field."

"I dinnae ken it, but I will find out. We must find her family and return her to them. I'm going to send some of the men to the village to ask if anyone there may know the family. Hopefully they werenae only passing through, but even if they were I believe we will find out." He sent one of the servants to get Taegen. If anyone could find the bairn's family, it was him. He was not only Aleck's captain, he was also his best tracker.

"Do ye think she may have fallen from the back of a wagon and it wasnae noticed?" Merry asked, tickling the bairn under the chin.

"Her family didnae want her or we wouldnae have found her," Isla said. She protectively tightened her arms around the wee one.

"Mayhap she was stolen from them and they are searching for her." Aleck paced back and forth before the fire. He had to solve this mystery before Isla became too attached to the child. He could already see it in her eyes and hear it in her voice.

Isla sat on the floor and took the bairn into her lap. She seemed quite the happy little one. Isla didnae consider herself to be the motherly kind, but something about this child touched her heart. She wanted to protect her and had a hard time believing that a good Ma and Da would leave their child alone or allow her to be stolen.

"Merry, we must have a name for her. What will it be?"

"She's nae ours, Isla."

This again. Honestly. Isla could not imagine why everyone had a problem with giving the wee one a name. "I ken it, but we must call her something." She thought about it and then came up with the perfect name. "She came to us in a storm. We should call her Gailleann."

Aleck rolled his eyes heavenward. She knew he thought her daft for wishing to name the child, but it felt right to do so.

"What do ye think of that little Gailleann?" she asked.

The bairn beamed happily at her, which made Isla smile. It was a real smile, something she hadn't been able to do since Derrick's death.

"Mama," Gailleann said. "Mama."

"She's calling ye Mama," Merry said.

"Aye. I heard her," Isla answered.

"Mayhap she's asking ye where her mother is?" Aleck suggested. Not receiving an answer from either sister, he said, "I'm going to gather me men. As soon as the weather clears we'll go in search of her parents." Aleck left them alone with the wee lass.

Isla purposely ignored him and continued chatting and playing with Gailleann.

"Her clothing is quite strange," Merry said, examining the knitted sweater Gailleann wore. It was a golden color with unusual buttons down the front and a hood which covered a mop of dark brown hair that matched the child's large, bright eyes. She fingered the buttons. "What is this made of? I've never felt anything like it."

Isla gave them a closer look, shrugging her shoulders. She had no idea. "Her wee shoes and socks are also very finely made, but her dress isnae like anything I've ever seen before."

"She must come from a noble family," Merry said.

Isla didn't wish to think about who or where her family might be. She chose to believe she had been left there for her as a gift from God.

"Lady Isla," one of the servants came into the great hall carrying something wrapped in leather. "The farrier has sent this fer ye."

"Oh, thank ye." Still holding Gailleann she jumped to her feet and went to him. "Give him my thanks, please and this." She handed him a pouch of silver.

"I will, m'lady." The servant handed her the sword and she examined it, holding it in one hand while holding the wee lass in the other arm. Gailleann seemed fascinated by the sword, which Isla deftly swung to and fro, never anywhere near the child. "Merry, will ye wrap this back up for me."

"Of course." Merry took it from her and carefully wrapped it. "What did ye have done with it?"

"I had it sharpened and polished."

"Derrick would be pleased ye've kept his sword."

"But would he be pleased that I use it?" Sadness settled in Isla's heart as she thought of Derrick, but it was different than it had been. The thought of him no longer brought with it gut wrenching pain as it had for so long.

"He would," Merry answered.

"How can ye be so sure?"

"Because he loved ye and if he knew how happy it made ye to learn how to use it, he would approve."

She gazed at the wrapped sword, she'd been feeling guilty for using it, but Merry's words brought her comfort. He would be pleased. She was sure of it. "I believe yer right. Would ye mind taking it up to me chamber? Maybe Aleck will have time tomorrow to practice with me."

"I'm sure he'd be happy to."

"Merry, someday I wish to find the men who murdered Derrick and when I do I plan to dispatch each and every one of them"

"Ye frighten me when ye speak like that. Ye cannae possibly imagine that ye alone can fight five men."

"I didnae say I would do it all at one time, but first I must find them."

Merry shook her head in dismay. "Killing those men willnae bring Derrick back, Isla. Ye must find a way to get on with yer life. I ken ye say ye wish to be alone, but I dinnae believe it. I know you better than anyone, sister. Ye've a loving heart. Ye should share it with someone."

"I dinnae have a heart as big as yers, Merry and I do prefer to be alone."

"Look how quickly ye've formed a bond with little Gailleann. Ye barely knew her for an hour and ye made her yer own."

"She is mine. Her family didnae want her," Isla argued.

"Her family is probably somewhere close by and searching for her. Wouldn't it be better if ye had a child of yer own to name?"

Isla didn't wish to continue this conversation. She glanced from Merry to the sword.

"I'll take this upstairs and when I return I'd like a chance to hold the bairn," Merry called over her shoulder as she left.

"Gailleann. Her name is Gailleann." Isla began dancing around the room with the bairn in her arms and Gailleann seemed to be enjoying it, laughing and clapping as they went. "Ye are a sweet little one, arenae ye?" She secretly hoped that her parents wouldn't be found, she'd only held her for a short while and couldn't imagine parting with her.

CHAPTER 15

"Isla, ye cannae keep the bairn," Aleck said for what felt like the hundredth time.

"What if ye cannae find her Ma and Da? Then surely I'll be able to keep her."

"That remains to be seen. My men are out searching the countryside from village to village. When they return, ye may have to give her up." He understood how she felt. He'd become quite attached to the wee lass in the week that she'd been with them.

"I willnae."

She was a stubborn one. She jutted her chin in the air and refused to look his way.

"Ye can have a child of yer own," he said.

"Nae. I cannae."

"Are ye barren?"

She appeared insulted by this. "I wouldnae ken it," she snapped.

"Then ye may verra well be able to have a child." He refused to give in to her nonsensical view of the way things should be.

"Nae."

"Why nae?" He was completely exasperated with her.

"I willnae marry, so I willnae ever have a child of me own."

"Isla, ye'd be a verra good mother." His tone softened. She would be a good mother. He could see it clearly.

Her response softened as well. "I believe I would. I didnae think I had it in me to nurture and care for a bairn. I never wanted to have a child if it couldnae be Derrick's bairn, but Gailleann has changed things."

"Has she now? Mayhap she can convince ye to marry." He realized he'd said the wrong thing as soon as the words left his mouth. He'd lit the fire of anger in her eyes once again.

"Dinnae make fun of me," Isla shouted." I can raise a child without need of a man. My family will help me," she asserted. She turned her back to him, her nose pointed proudly towards the ceiling.

He threw his hands in the air. She was the most maddening woman he'd ever met and yet she was also the most appealing. She was the one he wanted and the fact that she'd decided to live her life as if she were a nun was driving him mad. To top it all off, she'd once again announced to him that she wished to practice sword fighting with him and if he didn't have time, she would practice with his men. She even had her own sword. It had belonged to Derrick, but still he wondered what woman would have her own sword. Apparently, the kind of woman he was in love with. Heaven help him.

"What am I to do with ye?" he asked.

"Nary a thing, Laird." He hated when she called him Laird. She was purposely trying to irritate him and it was working.

"Ye wish to be this child's mother. Ye wish to practice with me men. Ye wish to find the men who murdered yer Derrick." *But yet ye dinnae wish to be me wife.*

"Aye. I wish to do all of those things. And I will."

He had no doubt she would. She was quite determined. "Ye may need some help with the last one."

"I may."

"I'd like to be the one to help ye, if ye'd allow it."

"I must find them first," she said. "I dinnae even ken who they are."

"I can help ye with that. When me men have found wee Gaille-ann's Ma and Da I'll have them start a search for the five ye seek."

He could see her jaw tighten at the mention of the bairn's family, but it wouldnae be right to keep her from her rightful parents unless of course they didnae want her, but he couldnae imagine that would be the case. She was a sweet wee lass. The only crying she'd done had been in the field where they found her. Since then she'd been quite happy.

Pierce Holmes stood on the outskirts of Sinclair Castle, far enough away that the guards wouldn't see him as he leaned against a large oak tree. He'd donned clothing he'd stolen from an unattended laundry basket in order to blend in. He didn't wish to draw attention to himself as he knew full well he'd been transported back in time. The remnants of the green light were all he had needed to make this journey. It was similar to the way he'd travelled the first time, when he'd come with Malcolm Granger to retrieve the sword. That time they'd been thwarted in their efforts by Edna Campbell, a witch from his own time. He was certain she wouldn't interfere this time, but if he had to kill her, he would. He had to get his hands on the sword. The legend he'd found among Malcolm's papers said that he needed two things. One was the blood of a Sinclair daughter. He hoped he'd chosen the right one, but the fact that she'd been stolen from him by some unearthly creature told him she was. She was here somewhere in this time and if there was one thing he knew, it was that she wouldn't be far from where he found himself now.

The other thing he needed was an emerald stone. Not just any emerald stone, but one that was in the safe keeping of a woman named Kat Mackall. He'd find that first and then he'd return here for the child. His gut was telling him she was in that castle and that she would be there until he returned for her. He was alone, but something was guiding him. He'd never been one to believe in psychic intuition, but lately he found himself going with his gut without question or pause. So far it had worked out. He was exactly where he needed to be to complete his mission. The voice inside his head told him to head West towards the setting sun.

"Any luck?" Aleck asked Taegen as they rode into the courtyard.

"Nae. We travelled to every village within a day's ride of here. None were missing a bairn."

"How can that be?" Aleck was quite perplexed. "She had to come from somewhere."

"Aye. But nae from anywhere nearby."

He tried to think of anything that would explain her appearance in the field, but the only thing that came to mind was that she'd been left there for a reason. She was left there to be found by him. Could it have been the elves who left her? The same elves who'd taken his sister away when she was but a wee lass. He knew they'd done it for her protection. Was that why this wee one had been left? If only there was a way to know for sure. He'd keep his thoughts to himself and wait for Nick and Kat to return. He hoped they might be able to shed some light on Gaileann's sudden appearance in their lives.

They should be back any time now. The feast was set for seven days time and it wouldn't do for the guest of honor to be missing. Every day that Gailleann stayed with them made Isla more and more attached to the wee thing. He was sure they'd find the parents and he dreaded the thought of having to take the child away from her when the time came. She'd suffered enough because of the death of her fiancé, losing this child might be more than she could bear. He'd be there for her, even though she didn't want him. He'd seen a different person these past days. She was laughing and smiling and not just when the babe was present. It gave him hope that she might reconsider her vow to never marry. The more time he spent with her, the more he knew he wanted to share his life with her.

Isla was falling in love with this wee lass. She knew it was a dangerous thing to do, but she couldn't help herself. Since Gailleann had appeared, Isla found that she was enjoying life once again. Her thoughts of Derrick had lessened. She knew she would never forget him, but she also knew that she couldn't dwell in the past any longer. There was so much life to be lived and she now knew she wanted to live it. She had to let go of the sadness she'd been bearing for so long now. It felt good to be happy. The tinge of guilt she'd felt at first had left. She'd been given a second chance and she was determined to make the most of it. "Isla, I'll take care of Gailleann for ye," Merry offered.

"Oh, there's nae need. I can stay with her." They were upstairs in Isla's bed chamber. Aleck had a cradle put in the room so she would never have to be too far from the wee one.

"I insist. Ye need to eat. Go. I can take care of her. I'd like to take care of her."

Isla hesitated, not wanting to go.

"Ye've been selfishly keeping her all to yerself. Let me do it, please," Merry pleaded.

"Alright. I won't be far and I'll be back as soon as I can."

"Isla, she's about to fall asleep. She willnae miss ye while she's dreaming."

"Yer right," Isla kissed Merry's forehead and did the same to Gailleann. "Good night, my love."

"Night," Gailleann said.

"She's a smart one," Merry said. "Ye've taught her so many new words."

Isla blew a kiss their way and both Merry and Gailleann returned it. She closed the door behind her and stood in the passageway for a moment thinking about how her world had changed so much in such a short time. Gailleann brought with her a joy that Isla didn't think she'd ever feel again. Her days now had a purpose. She was doing something she was much better at than she ever thought possible. She was caring for a bairn and even though the child wasn't Derrick's, she was drawn to her. She was finding that it was possible to live her life without Derrick. The world was filled with wonders she'd ignored and she couldn't help but imagine what else life might bring her way now that she willing to be open to it. She made up her mind right there in the passageway. She would give herself the gift of loving and being loved. She'd grieved a good long time for Derrick, it was time to move forward. She wouldn't allow her grief and sadness to stand in the way of her happiness any longer. Her tummy grumbled, reminding her that she was hungry and with a warm feeling in her heart she headed downstairs to the great hall where she was greeted by Aleck, who seemed to be waiting for her at the head table. He stood as she approached, holding out her chair for her while she sat.

"Are ye hungry?" he asked.

She nodded. "Verra. I've been so busy with Gailleann that I've forgotten to eat since this morning."

He broke off a piece of bread from a fragrant loaf, which sat in front of them and handed it to her.

"Thank ye," she said.

"Wine?"

"That would be lovely." For some reason she found herself blushing because of his attention.

One of the servants entered the room with plates of food for the both of them.

"Did Merry know ye were doing this?" she asked, suspicion tinging her voice as she noted that the hall was empty and that the two of them would be dining alone.

"Merry?" he asked, playing the innocent.

"Aye. She convinced me to leave Gailleann with her and come down to eat."

"Well, I'm happy she did." She gave him a sideways glance and he chuckled. "She may have had an inkling as to my intentions."

Isla took a bite of the bread and a sip of the wine. She was enjoying this. And why shouldn't she? Aleck was a gracious host and she found that she wanted to be near him. It went against everything she'd been telling herself since she'd arrived, but sitting next to him here, she could feel the warmth of his body emanating towards her. She liked it.

"The soup is delicious. Try some." He brought a spoonful of the broth to her lips, never taking his eyes from hers.

She sipped the broth. "Mmm… delicious."

She couldn't stop looking into eyes so green it was as if she were searching the depths of the ocean.

Next he offered her some cheese, touching her lips with his fingers as he placed it in her mouth. In the past, she would have quickly told him she was quite capable of feeding herself, but things had changed. She was enjoying this and wasn't about to tell him to stop. As a matter of fact, she thought she should join in by feeding him. She searched her plate for the right choice and decided on a fig. She offered it to him and he took the whole of it into his mouth, tasting her fingers with his lips. A small giggle left her lips and it was met by a deep chuckle from Aleck. She sipped her wine, taking the opportunity to enjoy the sight of this man she'd fought so hard to keep at arm's length. His long blond locks brushed past his broad, powerful shoulders. He looked up from his food as she placed her cup back on the table.

"What do ye see, Isla?" he asked.

"I see a man. A verra handsome man who has a kind and loving heart. A man who is a fair and strong leader."

"Ye've nae seen him before?" he asked, running his fingers along her jawline.

"I have, but I chose not to see him as he truly is. I was frightened of him." She was feeling quite relaxed here with Aleck. "What do ye see, Aleck?" she asked.

"I see a woman who has intrigued me from the verra first time I laid eyes on her. A woman whose heart is so big that she's felt the need to protect it from harm. A woman whose heart I would cherish and I would never harm. A woman whose past hasnae been easy, but whose future holds more than she could possibly hope for."

"Ye've seen this all along?" She was surprised by his words. She knew she'd been sharp tongued and difficult most of the time she'd known him. It amazed her that he saw beyond it.

The feelings running through her body were feelings which had been dormant for a long, long time. She wasn't sure where this would lead, but for now it made her happy. Aleck wanted her and he was doing his best to woo her. She had to admit, it was working

ALECK KNEW THAT he had to tread cautiously. Despite the fact that Isla seemed amenable to his advances, he knew if he wasn't careful she'd flee back to the safety of her room and shut her heart away once again. The sensual ritual of feeding each other was working its magic on both of them. He searched her face, expecting to see some sign that she wished him to stop, but instead he saw the same want he was feeling in his heart. A dribble of honey on her lips drew his mouth to hers, where her already sweet lips were now even sweeter. Soft, warmth mingled with hardened passion. They were alone. The servants had been dismissed. There was nothing holding them back. He tenderly lifted her from her chair into his arms, where she wrapped her arms around his neck, her hands deftly undoing the leather thong holding his hair back allowing her fingers to roam free through his golden locks.

"My chamber?" he asked, unsure of what her answer might be.

"Aye."

He carried her up the stairs and through the doors, setting her feet on the ground beside his bed which was covered in furs and big enough for two.

Isla stood on tiptoe, kissing Aleck's face and lips. His surprise at her forwardness was tempered by his need to have her. He continued to let her take the lead. If she was more comfortable with that, then so was he. Each kiss was followed by her explorations of his body. Her hands roamed over his chest and abs. She moved his shirt out of the way and the feel of her hands on his bare skin sent a shiver of pleasure through his body, hardening and readying his manhood. Aiding Isla in her quest to for skin-to-skin contact, he removed his shirt and she surprised him once again by leaving his lips behind and trailing kisses down his neck to his chest.

Aleck reached his hands around to her back, where he carefully undid the lacing of her dress. He dropped it off one shoulder, placing kisses where it had been only moments before. He wanted to go much further with his kisses, but he thought it best to be certain this was what Isla wanted.

"Are ye sure, love," he whispered in her ear.

"Verra," she answered.

She wasn't new to this, he understood and accepted it. There would be no shame in this for either of them. How lucky he was, when only a few short days ago he thought it completely impossible to woo Isla Mackall and yet now here she was in his arms and eager to be with him.

He kissed the sensitive spot at the base of her neck. Sweet, sweet sounds escaped her throat and he knew he was on to something. His hands fumbled with her dress and Isla took control. As she removed her dress he continued to assault her with kisses and small nips. His hands caressed her breasts and her waist. He wanted her beneath him... now.

His eyes took in this beautiful woman from head to toe. Her long dark tresses cascaded over her shoulders and down across her breasts. Isla wasn't shy. She didn't try to cover herself and he was glad of it. He pulled her close, running his hands across and down her back, cupping her buttocks. He wasn't sure he could control himself a moment longer, but Isla understood. She took his hand and backed herself up to the bed. There she carefully removed the rest of his clothing, taking her time and torturing him with the feel of her hands on his bare skin. When his clothes were off, Isla sat on the bed. Aleck lifted her more fully onto it and covered her with his large, strong frame. It was his turn to be in control. His large hands stroked her hair. Running his fingers down her neck and between her breasts, he watched Isla's reaction. He moved on to her belly, so silky soft and then further to the mound of curls that protected her womanly folds. As he neared her sensitive pearl, Isla moaned with pleasure and to his surprise and delight, opened her legs for him.

As a warrior, self-control was of the utmost importance and he found that same discipline coming in handy as he took pleasure in exploring Isla's body. He wanted to know every inch of it and was determined to make this first encounter between them memorable for her. He knew it would be for him.

As his fingers explored her heated sheath, she gasped audibly, followed by a satisfied, "Mmm…"

Aleck smiled. He was pleasing her. He continued lavishing her with kisses, his tongue darting between her lips to be met by the silky softness of her own. Her hands tangled in his curls. Every touch, every breath, every sound drove him onward. His only goal to satisfy this woman who was gifting him with her body.

Isla's decision to be with Aleck hadn't come lightly and now that she was experiencing the mastery of his love making, she could think of nothing more than Aleck. All her oaths and fears were set aside. She wanted him. She couldn't deny it any longer and she wouldn't. His sea green eyes gazed into hers and she felt herself melting into their intensity. She disentangled her hands from his silky, blonde locks, sliding them down his body, grasping his hard shaft and stroking. A low growl escaped him. As he was bringing her much pleasure, she wished to do the same for him. He rolled onto his back, taking her with him to lay across his chest. Hands on either side of her face, he lifted his head to kiss her lips. Long, languid kisses that caused an insistent thrumming to heighten her desire.

"Aleck," she breathed. "I want ye. Please dinnae think me a doxy."

"Never." He answered her with more kisses as he rolled her onto her back and placed his erection between her legs, teasing her as he entered her aching womanhood only to slowly depart. His nose touched hers as his teeth gently nipped her bottom lip. "Do ye want me, Isla?"

"Aye," she answered, her breath quickening and her heart beating wildly in her chest. "Aye."

He slid himself inside of her womanly warmth and moaned his pleasure.

Their coming together was filled with emotion and passion. Warm, wet, sensual, their bodies glistened with sweat. Aleck's thrusts became more insistent, touching Isla in all the right places. She floated on a sensual cloud, overcome with the need to reach the ultimate destination. She would get there with Aleck. He would take her. Crying out, her eyes opened wide, her body convulsing in pleasure that was doubled by the knowledge that Aleck was with her, calling her name as they both reached their ecstasy.

The beauty of what they'd shared wasn't lost on Isla. She wished it was something she could experience again and again, but as she lay next to Aleck, his arm thrown across her breast, she knew that she'd forgotten who she was. Forgotten what she vowed to herself. He deserved so much more than what she could give him and she couldn't bear the hurt she would suffer if anything happened to take him from her. It was best for her to go before she began to love him. She wasn't brave at all. She'd hated that word when she'd heard it from her friends and family after Derrick was gone. Her heart wasn't ready for this. She didn't know if it ever would be.

As quiet as she possibly could be, Isla moved from Aleck's side intent on escaping before she changed her mind.

ALECK FELT ISLA moving away from him. He reached for her, but she was already out of the bed and had gathered her clothing, holding it to her breasts as she hurried to the door.

"Isla, where are ye going?" he asked.

"I cannae do this, Aleck. I must leave." She opened the door and ran out into the passageway, leaving him alone in his bed.

"Isla!" he called after her, but it was no use. She was gone and he didn't understand why.

Their night of lovemaking had been perfect for both of them. He didn't question her reactions one bit. She enjoyed it as much as he. Aleck thought he'd gotten through to her, made a connection, but something had caused her to rethink her decision to be with him. Now he wondered if he'd experience the joy of having Isla Mackall ever again.

CHAPTER 16

A LECK RODE OUT alone. Time alone had always done him good in the past. He needed time to think. Isla hadn't shared breakfast with him. Merry joined him, but she said Isla wasn't feeling well and wished to stay in bed. He sent a tray of food up to her chamber and then, after finishing his own meal, took to his horse. Whenever something troubled him a good long ride on Brychan usually brought him answers. It didn't seem to be working today.

After being in the saddle for hours, Aleck dismounted near a small rill. He sat on its banks with a stick in hand tracing lines in the silty shoreline. A soft sound to his right caught his attention. He glanced up expecting to find a deer or rabbit, but instead was surprised to see a beautiful woman with long red locks and bright green eyes walking his way. He jumped to his feet, not sure if his eyes were playing tricks on him. Who was she? How had she gotten here? He quickly took stock of his surroundings, but all was quiet. They were quite alone.

"Aleck Sinclair, I am Anania, Queen of the Elves."

"Anania, the Elven Queen who took my sister from my family when she was but a bairn and then brought her back many, many years later?"

"The same." She sat on a nearby rock. "Please sit."

Aleck found a spot across from her and did as she requested. Of all the things he imagined could happen this day, meeting the Elven Queen wasn't one of them. He was awed by her ethereal beauty. "Why are ye here?" he managed to ask.

"I'm here to speak with ye about the bairn ye care for."

"Gailleann?"

"Her Ma and Da call her Molly. She has been placed in your care for safety sake. There is a man who would harm her in pursuit of the Twin Sword."

"But I saw that man die."

"The man died, but the sorcerer lives. He is weak, but has called a new disciple. Ariweth doesnae rest. He requires the sword and he has once again found a man to do his bidding."

"Where is the child's family?"

"They are in the future. Once the man is no longer a threat, she must be returned to them."

"Of course. What can I do to help?"

"Ye are already helping by caring for the wee one, but there may come a time when ye'll need to fight to defend her. I trust ye to do exactly that. 'Tis why she is with ye."

"But why me?"

"She is a Sinclair. Her Da is a Sinclair and another one who helps them is also a Sinclair."

"What?" This was unexpected news.

"She is yer many times great granddaughter." Aleck was stunned by this information. It seemed an impossibility that this wee lass was to be descended from his line. His mind was reeling with questions, but he could only ask, "So, I will have children?"

"Aye. Many. And they will have children, who will have children and so on. Your line will live on, but 'tis important that this man doesnae retrieve the sword – for your sake and for the sake of the generations to come."

"I will do whatever is necessary," he vowed. "They are mine to protect and I will do exactly that."

"Good. For now, yer only task is to keep the child safe. More may be required of ye in the future."

"Where is this man who threatens her?" He must find him. This child was of his blood and he would keep her safe. He would kill this man if necessary.

"Unfortunately, he is here in this time now. Although he is on his way to the home of the Mackall's in search of the emerald gem I left with Kat. He suspects Molly is here with ye and he will return."

Aleck's jaw muscle flexed as he balled his hands into fists. "He willnae get to her. I will see to it. But what about the Mackall's? I can send me men to warn them."

"No need. I will go. He will not retrieve the real emerald. Instead he will be given one that I have created especially for him." She smiled as she said this and Aleck wondered what she had planned for this man.

"Are the Mackall's in danger?"

"Nae. I will speak with Lettie Mackall. She will ken the reasons this man is there. She will give him what he wants and he will be on his way."

Aleck nodded his head. Anania seemed to have everything under control. He had some time before the man would return. Nick and Kat would be back soon and they would prepare for the arrival of this unknown enemy.

"I will leave ye now," Anania walked away from him, fading into a green mist as she did.

He'd best get back to the castle. He had to speak with Isla.

"I'M GOING TO take Gailleann out for some fresh air," Isla said as she adjusted the child's outer wrap. Thankfully, Merry was good with a needle. She'd managed to sew up several items of clothing for the wee lass to wear that were far more appropriate than what she'd been found in. "Do ye think she'll be warm enough?"

"She may be too warm based on the amount of clothing ye've put on her and the redness of her cheeks," Merry observed.

"Come, Gailleann. Let's go for a walk," Isla picked her up and carried her outside.

Gailleann squirmed in her arms and Isla set her down on the

ground, being sure to hold tight to her hand as they walked. Once or twice around the courtyard would be more than enough. Then she'd be ready for a nap.

"Isla," Aleck called as he rode up to them.

Gailleann seemed excited to see him, reaching her arms up towards him. Aleck hopped down from his horse and immediately picked her up, placing a kiss on her forehead. "Good morning, wee lass. Where are ye off to this fine day?"

"Mama?" Gailleann put her hands up and glanced around.

"Are ye searching fer yer Ma?" Aleck asked.

For the first time Isla realized that this little one was probably wondering where her mother and father were. She'd been so wrapped up in pretending she was her daughter that she never thought even for one instant that Gailleann might miss them.

"Who is this?" Aleck asked pointing at Isla.

"Isla," she said.

"Verra good. Who am I?"

"Sir," she said.

Aleck laughed heartily at this. She'd heard everyone addressing him as sir and thought that was his name. "Can ye say Aleck?"

"Aw weck," she responded.

"Verra good. 'Tis my name. Yer a smart wee one." He placed her back down on the ground where she reached for Isla's hand and then his. "I believe she'd like us both to take her for a walk. Do ye mind?"

Isla shook her head. She wasn't sure how to handle this. She'd made a mistake last night. Aleck was a good man and under any other circumstances, she thought she could easily love him, but this wasn't right. What if he was taken from her as Derrick had been? She simply couldn't go through that pain again. It had torn her apart to lose him and it wasn't until this visit with Aleck that the pain had begun to lessen. No matter that her belly did a little dance every time he was near and that her heart beat as swiftly as the wings of a hummingbird when he touched her. She'd had one night with him. One glorious night and that was all she would allow. Any more than that and she'd be unable to stop herself from falling in love with him.

"I would like to talk with you, Isla, it is important…" Aleck started

"Ah…last night." She interrupted him. "'Twas nothing. We were carried away in the moment. It cannae happen again, ye ken?"

Aleck seemed startled for a moment, then quickly recovered. "I dinnae *ken*. Isla, I wish it to happen again and again. I wish to have ye by me side always."

Isla shook her head, but could not bring herself to look at him, "That cannae be. I've made a pledge to meself that I willnae marry. I will nae break that pledge." Just saying the words out loud hurt her heart.

"Is it because of Derrick?" He asked. A tinge of bitterness in his voice.

She didn't answer.

"He wouldnae wish ye to waste yer life mourning his loss. He'd want ye to be happy." He stopped and turned her towards him. Little Gailleann stood between them gazing up.

"How do ye ken what he would wish?" she snarled. "He's dead. He cannae say."

Aleck did not flinch at her tone. Instead he held his ground, "Isla I'm nae asking ye to forget him. I'm only asking that ye give me a chance to make ye happy."

"I dinnae need ye to make me smile. I'm happy as I am." She was lying to him, and lying to herself. But if he knew how awful these past months had been for her, he'd know better than to believe he could be her savior. "If ye'll excuse us, we'll finish our walk and then Gailleann will need to rest."

She left him standing there with a sad, disappointed face. She wished it could be otherwise, but losing another love terrified her.

ALECK WAS UPSET and angry and unsure of what to do.

"Merry!" he yelled into the empty great hall. "Merry! Where are ye?" He paced back and forth before the hearth. Isla was the most obstinate, difficult woman he'd ever met and damn it, he loved her.

"Was that ye bellowing me name?" Merry asked as she approached.

"Aye," he snarled. Now he was starting to sound like Isla.

"What's wrong?" She stood, hands on hips before him. "From the looks of ye, I'd say Isla is what's wrong."

"Yer right."

"What's happened?"

"She's told me all about her Derrick. I never in a million years would imagine that I'd be jealous of a dead man, but I am."

Merry placed a calming hand on his forearm and he finally stood still. "Aleck, tell me what's happened. It must be more than just finding out about Derrick."

"Why did she nae tell me about him when I met her at Kat's wedding?"

"I'm nae sure. 'Tis something she doesnae speak of easily. At that time, I think she believed she should try to move on with her life. Ye ken the whole family always told her it was what she must do. She tried for a little while and then gave up. Isla was always a most determined lass. All her life, when there was something she wanted she worked and worked until she achieved it."

Aleck thought about her skill with a sword and what she must have gone through to develop the strength and skill needed to wield it. The other day at the stream, she hid her panic and went into the water rather than appear weak. He thought about how she had thrown herself into caring for Gailleann even though, at first, she was afraid to hold the babe. When she threw herself into a challenge she would not allow anyone, especially him, to stand in her way.

"When Derrick was murdered," Merry continued, "the one thing she wanted the most was taken from her and there was absolutely nothing she could do about it. Don't tell her I said so, but it made her fearful. She's always been afraid of the water, but this was different – she became afraid to live, afraid of love. Even afraid to love her own family."

Aleck thought about how Isla practically ran from the room last night. Was it fear of loving him that sent her scurrying away?

"Ye ken she was with me last night?" Aleck asked. It wasn't the most appropriate topic to bring up with Merry, but he had to speak with someone who understood Isla.

Merry glanced down at the ground, her cheeks reddening. "Aye."

"She left me in the middle of the night. Walked away and left me. Now she says we cannae be together ever again. She's made a vow never to marry. Do ye understand this?"

"Aleck, when Derrick was killed, Isla became a different person. She loved him so verra much and they were to marry within the month. The grief and pain she felt on losing him were devastating. We were all so worried for her. We didnae believe she would ever recover."

He listened intently, hoping Merry had the answer to this puzzle.

"Do ye nae ken that she fears it may happen again. She's afraid. By keeping her heart locked away, Isla believes she will never have to experience that pain again."

The lass made good sense. Why hadn't he seen it? "Is there nae a thing I can do then? Is this the way it must be?"

"I dinnae believe it must be this way. Be patient with her. Keep being the kind and good-hearted man that ye are. She has feelings for ye, of that I'm certain. But she'll guard them. Ye must allow her to decide on her own. Given time, I believe she will."

Aleck hoped Merry was right. His feelings for Isla had been growing since he'd first set eyes upon her. He knew in that very first meeting that she'd be his wife, but apparently Isla had other plans and they didn't include him or any other man. "Ye are a wise woman, Merry."

"I ken it," she smiled, a glint of mischief in her eyes. "Shall we go over the plans for the feast?"

He nodded and wrapped an arm around her shoulders, pulling her close for a hug. "Thank ye."

"I'll get cook and we'll tell ye everything we've planned. Have the invitations gone out?"

"They have. I believe everyone will come."

She clapped her hands, obviously elated and spun on her heels to go in search of cook.

ALECK FOUND ISLA in the great hall playing with Gailleann. He wasn't sure what kind of reception he'd receive from her, but he had to speak with her.

"Isla, there's news ye must hear," he announced right away. The last thing he wanted was for her to walk away form him again.

"Is something wrong?" she immediately pulled Gailleann into her lap.

"Aye." He hesitated, not wanting to say too much, but knowing he had to tell her about his meeting with Anania.

"Well…" Her stern expression told him she was still angry with him, but he couldn't wait for her to forgive him before speaking about this.

"I was out riding today and I was visited by the Elven Queen, Anania. I'm sure ye've heard of her."

"I have, but I've never seen her," she said, a bit of skepticism in her voice.

"She told me that Gailleann is from the future. She was brought here to us to keep safe."

"From what?" Isla's reaction to this news wasn't as he'd expected. If she had her sword, he imagined her jumping to her feet to protect Gailleann.

"There's a man from the future, who wishes her harm. He is

here now in our time."

Before he could finish, Isla jumped up from the floor, holding Gailleann in her arms. "I must get me sword. I cannae allow him to harm the bairn." She headed for the door.

"Isla! Wait! There's more and I wish you to hear it. I too would love nothing more than to find this poor excuse for a man and run him through, but we cannae. He's on his way to Dunnet Head to retrieve an emerald stone that has been in Kat's keeping. We must wait for him to come to us. And he will."

"Shouldn't we warn me family that he's coming?" "Anania has vowed to do it. She has a plan. No one in your family will come to any harm. She will give him a replica of the gem Kat keeps and then he will come here in search of Gailleann."

"I'll be ready for him."

"We'll be ready for him." This warrior woman was having an unusual effect on him. He found her quite arousing and made up his mind in that moment to court Isla, whether she liked it or not.

"We should join forces and keep Gailleann with us at all times. It will be easier to keep her safe," he said, feeling just a wee bit guilty for using the child to get what he wanted.

"Aye. Yer right," she said, surprisingly agreeing with his plan.

Aleck intended to woo her by showing her what a good protector and provider he could be. There was no time like the present. He would start right away. He would help with Gailleann. He would take them both for walks and he would do his best not to say or do anything that would upset their new-found peace.

THE FOLLOWING DAYS were filled with preparations for the feast, but through it all, Aleck was sure to be by Isla's side. He was sure she would tire of his attention, but she seemed to be tolerating him quite well.

"I'm going to bring Gailleann upstairs for a nap," Isla said as they entered the castle after their morning walk.

"Allow me to do it," Aleck said. He was already holding Gailleann in his arms and he found that he wanted to hold her close for a little while longer. He'd grown quite attached to her.

Isla nodded her approval and they climbed the stairs to her chamber. By the time they reached her cradle, the bairn was sleeping comfortably with her head resting on Aleck's chest. Isla smiled sweetly at them as Aleck gently lowered the wee lass into her bed. She never stirred and he proudly felt it was a great accomplishment.

Isla held her finger to her lips and walked out to the passageway. "She'll sleep for a while now," she said, her voice just above a whisper.

"What will ye do?" he asked.

"I think I'll rest for a while. I'm sure ye've got many lairdly things to attend to," she teased.

"Yer right. I do." He didn't wish to leave her and wondered what he could do to avoid it. "I'm concerned that Nick and Kat willnae return in time for Kat's own feast."

"They'll be back," she assured him. "Nick will be sure of it." She stood in the doorway, her hand on the door. "We'll find ye when she wakes." Much to Aleck's disappointment, she closed the door in his face.

CHAPTER 17

T HAT NIGHT, JUST two days shy of the feast, Kat and Nick came riding into the courtyard followed by Nick's men and a cart loaded with goods they had purchased in Edinburgh.

"Welcome back," Aleck said, scooping Kat down from her horse and hugging her tightly. "I'm so happy ye've returned. Sister, what did ye think?"

"It was amazing! Exactly as I imagined it would be. We've brought gifts for everyone." She kissed his cheek, and returned his hug.

"I didn't think ye'd get back in time," Aleck said to Nick, who had just finished dismissing his men.

"I cannae believe ye doubted me," Nick said, clapping Aleck on the back.

"Much has happened since ye've been gone," Aleck informed him.

"Does it involve Isla?" Kat asked, eyes alight with anticipation.

"Not completely."

"Are ye to be married?" Nick asked.

"Nae."

Disappointed faces stared back at him.

"'Tis nae fer lack of trying," Aleck assured them.

"So ye still want her?" Nick asked, sounding hopeful.

"Unfortunately, I do."

"That doesnae sound good," Nick said.

"I'll do me best to explain."

Aleck escorted them to the great hall, where he gave them warm cider and seats before the hearth.

"I hardly know where to begin."

"Start with Isla," Kat suggested.

"Alright. She has informed me that she doesnae wish to marry anyone, but I havenae given up on her yet. I've been close a time or two, but I cannae imagine my life without her."

"Good. There are no quitters in our family, Aleck," she informed him with a bright smile.

He couldn't help but chuckle at her pronouncement. He continued on, telling them about finding little Gailleann and about Anania's warnings. When he was finished, a dazed Nick stared back at him.

Kat took control of the conversation from here. "Well, it seems there's much to do. We should prioritize and focus on what needs to be done. First, the threat to Dunnet Head is minimal. Nick, your warriors are well trained and will make sure that the clan is safe. Second, we will make preparations to keep the child safe. Third, do not give up on Isla, Aleck. We're here to help. Just let us know what you need."

At times like these, Aleck could see where Kat's growing up in the future was definitely to their benefit.

"I am worried about Isla. She's become incredibly attached to Gailleann. I'm afraid that when she must return to the future and to her parents that it will all be too much for Isla. She's only recently begun to let go of the grief she's felt from losing Derrick."

"She told ye about it," Nick said, clearly astonished. "She's never spoken to me about it. I had to hear it from me mum and then I was sworn to secrecy, which is why I never said anything to ye."

"I understand," Aleck assured him. "'Tis good to ken ye are a man who can be trusted."

"Do ye mean to tell me that ye didnae ken it already?" Nick feigned injured feelings.

"Nevertheless, ye cannae give up on her," Kat said.

"I dinnae intend to."

"Good. I'll talk with her about Gailleann."

"I'm still concerned about this man ye told us of. He was going to Dunnet Head to retrieve the emerald," Nick said.

"Anania assured me that all would be well. She would see to it that he received a replica of the gem and then he will return here for the child."

"I thought this threat had been taken care of," Kat said, sounding worried.

Aleck knew that it hadn't been so very long ago that Kat had her own run in with a man who was after the Twin Sword. They'd killed him and thought all was well. How wrong they all were.

"Aleck would it be possible for a man to get a real drink? Enough with this warm cider." Nick pushed the cider aside, making a face, which had Kat laughing.

"Of course. He walked to the table and picked up the flask of whisky and two quaichs. He poured whisky for Nick. Kat shook her head when he offered her a quaich.

"We'll be ready for him." Nick sipped his whisky. "Will Anania let us know he's on his way?"

"I believe she will."

"I'm going to find yer sisters. I want to meet this little lass that has captured Isla's heart," Kat caressed her husband's face and then left them.

"I'm a lucky man," Nick said, watching her walk away.

"Yer both lucky," Aleck said, wishing that his own luck would somehow change.

Isla and Merry were seated on the floor with little Gailleann between them. They were playing with a small wooden ball that Aleck had fashioned for her. Gailleann would roll the ball to one and then the other sister, laughing each time.

The door opened and Kat walked in much to the surprise of the two women. Merry jumped up from the floor and almost knocked Kat over with excitement as she threw her arms around her.

"Yer back!" Merry exclaimed.

"I am. I've come to say hello to ye both and to meet this little one." She joined Isla on the floor. "Hello," she said, reaching out a hand to touch Gailleann's face. "Yer a beauty." She placed an arm around Isla, hugging her.

"I'm happy to see ye," Isla said. "This is Gailleann."

"Aleck told me all about how ye found her. An incredible tale, but one that I'm rather familiar with."

"I'd almost forgotten that ye were taken from yer family as a wee lass."

"Aye. I was. I was quite young, as is little Gailleann. I didn't remember anything about my real family, but I know they never forgot about me. I cannae imagine how difficult it must have been for them to have lost a child."

Isla felt a pang of guilt as she listened to Kat's story. "I wish I had been able to grow up here at Castle Sinclair with the love of me own Ma and Da, and Aleck of course." Kat held her hand out and Gailleann took it. "She's a lovely, wee lass. I imagine her Ma and Da miss her terribly. Ye ken she'll have to return to them, dinnae ye, Isla?"

Tears formed in Isla's eyes and she brushed them away. "I cannae let her go," she said.

"But ye must. 'Twould nae be fair to Gailleann or her family."

"I wish to go with her," Isla said, her voice cracking with emotion. "I cannae let her go alone."

Kat's soft reassuring voice was like a balm to Isla's wounded soul. The words she was saying were not the words that Isla wished to hear, but Kat was right. She had to allow Gailleann to go home.

"I will go with her," she said again. Her voice gaining strength.

"I dinnae believe that will be possible, Isla," Kat explained.

"I willnae let her go unless I can go with her." Her heart was breaking once again. The pain she'd somehow managed to dispell when this wee one appeared in that field was back. Her heart hurt with old pain.

"To what end?" Kat asked. Her voice was soft and conveyed concern.

"I must see with my own eyes that her family truly wants her. If they dinnae, then I will keep her."

"Ye'll have to convince Anania," Kat said.

"I will. I have to."

Gailleann seemed to understand that Isla was sad. She came to her and sat in her lap and rested her head on her breast. Isla held her close, not wanting to think about losing this beautiful bairn.

"And what of Aleck?"

At the mention of Aleck's name, Isla realized if she went to the future, she'd be leaving him behind. Was this why Kat was asking. "What of him?"

"Do ye care for him?" Kat asked, brushing a wayward strand of hair from Isla's face.

"Of course, I do." She did care for him, more than she thought possible. She'd come to welcome his presence in her life and missed him when he wasn't near.

"He cares for ye as well." Kat's soft voice touched a chord in Isla.

"I cannae do it again. The pain is too much…" Isla began to cry. The first real cry she'd had since Derrick passed. A flood of tears ran down her cheeks. All the pain she'd kept locked inside emerged in those tears. Sobs wracked her body.

Little Gailleann squirmed from her arms and stood in front of her. She placed her hands on either side of Isla's face. "Nae cry," she said. She put one little finger to her lips. "Shhh…"

Merry and Kat put their arms around Isla and Gailleann. They all sat there as Isla cried every single tear she'd held inside for such a long time. Merry rested her head on Isla's shoulder as Kat rubbed her back.

"Let it all out, love," Kat murmured. "Let it all out."

They sat that way for what seemed like hours before Isla became silent. She wiped her eyes on her sleeve.

"You needed that," Kat said, handing her a hankie she'd tucked inside her sleeve.

"I ken it." A lot of things became clear to her as she cried. She'd loved Derrick so verra, verra much, but he was gone and being alone for the rest of her life wouldn't protect her heart from losing others she loved. She also understood that Aleck was in pain and she was the cause of it. He cared deeply for her and she had hurt him with her words and her actions. She wasn't sure she could ever make it up to him or if he would even want her now. "I must speak with Aleck."

"We'll take care of Gailleann," Merry said.

"I must look a sight," she said.

"Come, splash some cold water on yer face," Kat led her to the basin and filled it with water.

Isla rinsed her face. "I hope he willnae notice I've been crying."

"And what if he does? 'Twill let him know ye are human," Kat said.

Isla was so appreciative to have the benefit of her wisdom. "I missed ye," she said. She had gotten into the habit of giving everyone the impression that she didn't need any of them. That was all about to change.

Kat smiled warmly, brushing a few wet strands of hair from Isla's face. "Yer perfection and ye ken it."

Isla glanced down at her drab grey dress and wondered how anyone could think that true. "Can ye help me change into something a bit more colorful?"

"I'd be happy to. Merry, what dresses have ye brought with ye?"

"Oh, I know just the one. 'Twill look lovely on ye," Merry said, rising from the floor and heading to the wardrobe. Gailleann followed along behind her. She pulled a sage green dress with gold trim around the neckline and belted waist. The sleeves were lined with the same gold fabric. She brought it to Isla, with Gailleann trailing behind holding onto the train of the dress.

Kat and Merry helped Isla change into the gown and then fixed her hair. It had been so long since she'd cared what she looked like.

"Do ye think Aleck will be pleased?" she asked.

"I do," Kat said.

"One more thing." Merry retrieved a jeweled necklace from a box in the wardrobe. "Turn around and I'll put it on ye." When Merry was finished, Isla turned to look at her. "Ye look so beautiful." She placed her fingers to her lips. "You're going to make him so happy."

"I hope so."

"I'll go down with ye. He's speaking with Nick."

As they approached the great hall, Kat motioned for Isla to stay put while she entered the hall. "Nick, may I see ye for a moment, please?"

He turned to see her and immediately stood. "I'll return shortly."

"Take yer time," Aleck said.

ALECK TURNED BACK to the fire, wondering how things had turned out this way. There was a feast to plan and a madman due on his doorstep soon, but tonight all he could think about was Isla.

"Aleck?" the sweet sound of Isla's voice reached his ears as though he had conjured her with his thoughts.

He spun around to see her standing close enough that he could easily have pulled her into his arms, but he didn't. He was sure she wouldn't want that. Something had happened though. She was no longer dressed in her drab grey garb. There was a light in her eyes as if the burden she'd borne for so long, the one that had extinguished the light, had left her. She was even more beautiful than he'd thought her to be all along.

"Are ye nae going to say anything?" she asked.

He found his voice. "I…" Before he could utter another word, she was in his arms. Her soft warmth penetrating his uncertainty.

"I'm so sorry." she said.

"Sorry? Why?" he asked, unsure of what had happened to bring her to this point.

"I'm sorry I've been so terrible to ye. If ye dinnae hate me too much, I'd like to have another chance."

Aleck tightened his arms around her. "Isla, I could never hate ye. Yer too special to me."

A brilliant smile burst onto her upturned face. "I've been afraid."

"I ken it." Happiness shot through him. Isla was here in his arms, letting him see her vulnerability.

"Will ye be patient with me?" she asked, now becoming the one who was uncertain.

"Happily. May I kiss ye?"

"Please." She gazed up at him with eyes of the deepest brown. Eyes he could get lost in they were so beautiful.

He tenderly framed her face with his hands as he dipped his head to place a kiss on the sweetest of lips. Her response shot through him. He ached for more, but he would take things slowly, at her pace.

CHAPTER 18

T HE CASTLE WAS buzzing with activity. The feast was to take place later this day and guests were already arriving. The doors to the castle had been opened since sunrise. The servants were busy taking care of horses, carriages and guests. Rooms were prepared for those who would be staying overnight. Food was served to hungry travelers and to castle residents alike. Aleck was pleased with everything. This was his sister's day and it was going to be perfect. He'd waited his whole life to do this for her.

"Can I help with anything?" Kat asked of her brother.

"Nae. Everything has been taken care of, sister. This is yer celebration. Ye've nary a thing to do but enjoy it." Aleck was beaming.

"Ye seem quite happy this morning," Kat observed, matching his bright smile with one of her own.

"I am." In fact, he couldn't be happier. Everything seemed to be going his way.

"Would Isla be the reason for your smiling face?" she teased.

"I believe ye ken the answer, but aye, she is." He chucked his sister under the chin.

"Be good to her, brother," she said, her voice growing serious.

"How could ye believe I'd be anything but," he replied, shaking his head in wonder at her comment.

"I'm teasing ye. I ken yer a good man."

"Shall we go greet our guests?" He reached for her hand and she followed him out to the courtyard where more people were arriving.

They wandered through the crowd of people and Aleck introduced her to anyone she didn't know. She was already familiar with many of them, but there were a few newcomers.

"Everything is going as planned," he proudly said. "I've Merry to thank for that."

"She was delighted to assist ye. She is a good help to Nick and her Ma back at Dunaill."

"I imagine she is. Speaking of Merry, there she is." He waved her over to join them.

Merry's excitement was clear to see as she hurried to greet them. "Good day, Aleck... Kat."

"Good day."

"'Tis so exciting! Almost everyone is here." She glanced around obviously pleased and proud to see everything going so smoothly. "Will ye be taking part in the horse races this afternoon?"

"Aye. I can hardly wait." Aleck said. He waved to a couple coming in through the gates and they returned his greeting.

"Nick will race as well," Kat said.

"I was expecting an easy win, now I'm nae so sure," Aleck teased.

"Ye should be worried. Nick's horse is quite fast."

"As is mine," he responded.

"After the horse races, we've games planned for the rest of the day and then the feast," Merry said.

"Where is Isla?" Aleck asked.

"With Gailleann," Merry said.

"I'm going to go see if I can help her so she can join us for some fun," Kat said. "Will we find ye here when we return?"

"I'll be somewhere nearby," Aleck said.

"Ye'd be hard to miss," she teased. Kat squeezed his hand and then walked back towards the keep.

Several of the villagers had set up shop in the outer courtyard, selling everything from jewelry and fabric to meat pies. They had attracted quite a crowd. Aleck didn't recognize everyone, but then he hadn't expected to. Invited guests would naturally bring along an entourage of servants and soldiers who would be given time to enjoy themselves as well.

Aleck's good friend, Will approached with his wife and three little ones. He greeted them, giving each of the children coin to purchase a sweet from one of the tables filled with every kind of baked good ye could imagine.

"What do ye say, lassies?" Will asked them.

"Thank ye, Sir Aleck," their sweet little voices sang.

"Yer ma will take ye while I speak with Sir Aleck." They waved at their Da as they headed off. "I've nae seen so many people here in a verra, verra long time."

Aleck looked around at the happy crowd. The smell of meat cooking on a spit nearby had his mouth watering. A large group of children were being amused by a juggler near the entrance to the keep. All around him people were laughing and enjoying themselves. "There's been no reason to celebrate until now."

"Let's hope there be many more opportunities in the future."

They walked past those standing in line for drinks and food.

"Laird!" a young serving woman came up to them carrying a tot of whisky for each of them.

"Thank ye," Aleck said and then turning to Will, "To good friends."

"I'll drink to that." Will drank to his friend's toast.

"Are ye racing today?" Aleck asked.

He nodded his head. "Are ye?"

"Aye."

"Then mayhap I willnae," Will joked.

Aleck placed a hand on his shoulder. "'Twould no be a real race without ye." he said honestly.

"Dinnae fear. I'll be there and I intend to win."

Pierce Holmes walked into the courtyard unnoticed. This had been the perfect day for him to arrive. Luck was definitely on his side. Now he merely needed to wait for the right moment to present itself and he'd be off with the child. No one here knew who he was, but with so many others wandering around the courtyard, he didn't think it would be a problem even if they did. Getting the gem at Dunnet Head had been easier than he thought. He merely had to pay one of the servants to steal it for him. They were eager to help once they knew they'd be paid handsomely for their effort. He remained on the outskirts of the castle and waited overnight. The next morning, the servant returned with the gem hidden in a cloth bag. The man assured him that no one had seen him and that they wouldn't notice the gem missing for quite sometime. It had been locked away in his master's chamber and they were away visiting family.

Pierce paid him and then asked the man to get him a horse. "'Twill cost ye more than ye've already given me," the man said.

"Fine. The horse had best be fast and strong."

The man nodded and left him, returning shortly with a horse who seemed unable to keep his feet on the ground. "What is this?"

"Ye said ye wanted a horse that was fast and strong. This one fit yer request."

PIERCE HAD A few days on the road with his new mount and they managed to come to an agreement of sorts. Pierce wouldn't try to hold the horse back and the horse, in turn, wouldn't throw him. Not the best arrangement, but by the time they reached their destination, both horse and rider seemed to be in sync.

"May I take yer horse, sir," a young lad approached him from the stable area.

"No, I'll keep him with me, if you don't mind."

"I dinnae mind, sir. Are ye planning to ride in the race?" the lad asked.

"Race?"

"Aye, sir. There'll be a race this afternoon. Laird Sinclair and his guests will participate."

"Will there be a prize for the winner?" If there was, he was definitely going to race. If he was going to be here much longer, he could use the funds he'd receive to sustain himself until he could get to the sword.

"I believe so, sir."

"Good, then I will race." Pierce walked away with his horse, who suddenly had suddenly become a lot more valuable to him.

Kat and Nick were enjoying some time at the stalls set up in the outer courtyard.

"Havenae ye spent enough on trinkets while we were in Edinburgh," Nick teased.

"I did, but I like to look," she said as she fingered a lovely blue velvet cape.

"I'll buy it for ye if ye like," he said, wrapping a loose curl of her hair around his finger. He loved to please his wife. The blue velvet cape would shine on her. She was a true beauty and in his eyes, no one else could compare.

Kat gazed into his eyes and he felt movement beneath his kilt. She smiled, and touched his lips, knowing full well what she was doing to him. "I believe ye'd buy me the Taj Mahal if ye could," she laughed, moving on to another stall.

"The Taj what?" he asked, following close behind and appreciatively squeezing her bottom.

She playfully swatted his hand away. "Never mind. It's a saying from my time."

Nick tickled her ribs and enjoyed the squeal she let loose, causing everyone in the area to look their way.

"Nick!" she cried. As she spun to face him, she stopped suddenly, looking over his shoulder.

Nick followed her gaze. "What is it, love?"

"That man looks familiar, but I'm not sure where I know him from." She was standing on tiptoe now to get a better look.

"Hmmm…" Nick thought he looked familiar as well.

"Perhaps we saw him in Edinburgh," she said.

"I don't know. Would we have seen him when we were at court?"

"'Tis possible."

"We should go introduce ourselves," Nick said, taking her by the hand and heading towards the man, but before they'd moved too far, the man disappeared into the crowd. "He's gone. I wonder who he is?"

"I'm sure it will come to me."

ALECK WAS LINED up alongside Nick, Will and the other riders at the starting line of the race just outside the castle walls. It would be run through the countryside along a track marked by flags and would lead the riders through trees, flatland and hills eventually ending back at the starting line. The men around them were spouting good natured insults at one another as they waited for the signal to begin. At Merry's suggestion, members of the castle staff stood along the route to help with any misfortune which may befall the riders. Everything about the celebration had been planned with precision, thanks to her.

"Are ye ready?" Nick asked.

"Ready to beat ye? Certainly," Aleck said.

"We'll see about that," Will said.

"Ye'll be seeing nothing but my horse's arse, my friend."

Will chuckled at this and Aleck joined him. All three enjoyed a good challenge and all three liked to win, though they had agreed that should one of them come in first, they would not accept the prize. Instead the money would go to the second place finisher.

He could see Kat, Merry, and Isla on a small rise near the starting line. Gailleann was smiling and clapping in Isla's arms. He waved to them and watched as Isla and the bairn blew kisses in his direction. His heart swelled at the sight and he knew that no one would be able to beat him this day.

The stable master approached the starting line. The horses pranced in place, ready to be set loose. There was a hush among the bystanders who stood alongside the starting line waiting patiently for the race to begin.

"Are ye ready?" called the stable master.

A loud, "Aye!" came from the riders.

"Set!"

The riders got in position.

"Ride!" He waved a flag, signaling the beginning of the race and the riders were off, flying from the start and bolting down the track. Aleck and Nick were neck and neck as they left sight of the castle. Will wasn't far behind.

Once out of sight of the castle, the riders spread out with Nick, Aleck, and Will out in front. The others had fallen back and although they were still trying desperately to catch up, it didn't appear they'd be able to. Aleck peeked back over his shoulder and was surprised to see a rider catching up with them. The man blew past, holding onto an obviously out-of-control horse. Aleck had never seen a horse run so fast in all his days. He was leaving them in the dust. He glanced at Nick, who looked at him and nodded. They put their heads down and along with Will, urged their horses on as they attempted to catch up.

BACK AT THE finish line, the crowd cheered the incoming riders on.

"There's Nick and Aleck!" Kat said. "Who's the man in front of them?"

"I dinnae ken. 'Tis hard to see his face."

The riders blew past them in a cloud of dust. The women covered their noses and mouths so as to not inhale the dust. Isla covered Gailleann's face with the hood of her cape, pulling it down low. The wee lass tried desperately to get it out of her face so she could see what was going on. Isla walked back away from the finish line and the flying debris.

She pulled away the hood and cooed, "There ye be," to Gailleann, who giggled at this new game they were playing. She pulled the hood down again and Isla peeked inside to see Gailleann hiding with her eyes closed. "Do ye believe that if ye cannae see me I cannae see ye?" She tickled her belly.

Gailleann shrieked with delight. "Come, let's go see who's won the race."

They walked back to the finish line where Aleck was awarding the bag of silver to the winner. His hood was pulled low over his face, so it was impossible to see him, but he readily accepted his prize, holding it in the air for a moment for the crowd to see before taking his horse and walking away.

"Who was that?" Isla asked Aleck.

"No one I've ever seen before. He must be here with one of our guests."

"His horse was faster than yers," she noted.

"The horse was on his own. The rider was barely holding on. He didnae ride like a man who knew what he was doing."

"But still he won," she teased.

"That he did," Aleck chuckled. He smiled down at Isla and Gailleann who, as always, was happily watching everyone and everything. "What of ye, little lass. Are ye having fun?"

She looked up at him with those big brown eyes and melted his heart. He remembered what Anania had told him and knew that he would be a father. He hoped his children would be as happy as little Gailleann seemed to be. He then gazed at Isla. He knew she would be heartbroken when it was time to return the child to her parents, but it couldn't be helped. He decided not to think about it for the moment. Right now everything was fine and, coward that he was, he preferred to keep it that way.

CHAPTER 19

ISLA WAS EXCITED to participate in the afternoon activities. She dressed in her practice garb, braided her hair and grabbed her newly sharpened sword. She'd never participated in anything like this before and she was excited to do so. People who were milling around the courtyard, stopped and stared as she passed. She knew they weren't used to seeing a lass dressed for battle, but she wouldn't let anything dampen her spirits today. The rules of the competition were simple. She needed to best every opponent she came up against to win. She was confident she could do it and was so focused on her own thoughts that she didn't realize the practice field had gone silent until she looked up to see Aleck Sinclair striding towards her with an angry glare on his face.

"Isla, what are ye doing?" he took her by the arm and guided her back the way she'd come, but she pulled free of him.

"I'm going to take part in the mock battles," she said, glaring right back at him.

"I dinnae believe that to be a good idea."

"I don't care." She was digging her heels in. "You know I am a great fighter."

"These men wouldnae be comfortable fighting with a woman."

Standing her ground, she took in a huge breath and narrowed her eyes at Aleck. "Ye cannae tell me what to do!" she shouted.

"I can and I have." They were nose to nose now, neither of them giving any ground to the other.

Isla spotted her brother Nick, who was headed their way at a jog. "Isla, what are ye up to?"

"I wish to take part in the mock battle," she answered, still staring daggers at Aleck.

"Isla, we're nae at home now. Aleck is our host and if he doesnae believe it to be a good thing for ye, then I agree with him."

"Grrr..." She was so angry she could spit. It was going to be embarrassing to walk away, but she didn't wish to ruin Kat's day by causing a scene. So, she quietly turned and walked back to the castle. She thought Aleck had accepted her as she was, but she could see that was not to be the case. She couldn't possibly be with a man would didn't respect her right to use a sword. She marched back up to her chamber where Merry waited with the bairn.

"Yer back so soon," Merry noted.

"Aye. Aleck told me I couldnae fight." She plunked herself down on the edge of the bed.

"He did?" Merry seemed incredulous.

"Can ye believe it?" she threw her arms in the air and paced around the room, swinging her sword as though Aleck was in front of her.

"I think I can. The competition would bring in men from all over, they wouldn't know how to fight with a woman."

"Ye fight a woman just like ye fight a man!" Isla yelled. She was angry about missing the chance to practice her skills in a real competition. But she was also hurt. "He embarrassed me in front of all the other guests."

"I'm sorry."

"I believe I'll stay here, Merry. Ye can go mingle with the guests."

"Isla, dinnae do that."

"I'm doing it. Dinnae ye start telling me what to do."

"Alright. Mayhap ye'll change yer mind?"

"I dinnae believe so. Go. I want to be alone."

"Do ye wish me to take Gailleann?"

"Nae. I'll keep her with me."

Merry quietly closed the door behind her as she left. Isla was fuming mad. At home, she was allowed to do whatever she liked. She had no intention of being with a man who thought he could tell her what to do. Especially when it came to things she loved.

"Ye've done it now," Nick said.

"I ken it." Aleck knew he'd done the wrong thing. It was just that most of the men here would see it as inappropriate for her to battle them and he also feared she would be injured.

"Yer going to have a hard time making it up to her."

"Nick, I merely did what I thought best. I dinnae mind if she practices with the men, but to partake in this competition with men who wish to win at all costs... I couldnae allow it."

"Do ye love her?" Nick asked.

"I..." Aleck couldn't seem to get the words out. He believed he did love her, but he wasn't sure how she felt about him and he worried that she would only end up walking away from him. Especially now.

"If ye do, ye need to understand that Isla is filled with a passion for life. She has kept it hidden inside since the loss of her fiancé. The only way she's expressed it has been by learning to become a good warrior. If ye havenae seen her wield a sword, I'm sure ye have nae idea how good she is."

"I have seen her."

"Then you understand."

"I owe her an apology. I've really mucked things up."

"Ye did. But ye can make it up to her later. Right now, we have to get out there and show them what a real warrior fights like."

Aleck smiled warmly at Nick. He was a good man to know and an even better man to have on yer side.

They waded into the fray and battled their friends and neighbors. The rules were simple. Once you lost your sword or found yourself at the end of your opponent's you were to leave the field. As combatants tired, the numbers diminished until there were only two left.

"Me arms feel as heavy as tree trunks," Nick said, heaving his swords in Aleck's direction.

"Mine are the same." Aleck deflected Nick's sword with a blow of his own.

Unsurprisingly it would be Aleck or Nick who would end up the winner. The last two men they'd fought would be given the prize, but they would have satisfaction of being the last man standing. Somehow over the course of their sole battle, they ended up at the end of the other's sword. The crowd hooted with laughter. It seemed a fitting end. A tie. The two men hugged each other and then fell to the ground from exhaustion.

Laying next to each other in the dirt, Nick said, "If ye thought that was hard, wait until ye try to speak with Isla. I dinnae envy ye."

"Exactly what I wanted to hear," Aleck chuckled.

AFTER BATHING AND putting on clean clothes, Aleck entered the great hall to greet their guests as they came in for the feast in honor of his sister Kat. Familiar faces of old friends were a welcome sight. He spoke with each of them, asking after their families and themselves. It wasn't just the act of a host making his guests feel welcome, he was truly interested in the lives of his clan members and neighbors. Once they'd spoken with him, they made their way to their seats. The tables began to fill and the room hummed with conversation. The servants wound their way through the room serving ale and wine. Candles and torches were lit, giving the room a golden glow. Musicians stood in the far corner, playing softly so as not to interfere with the guests who were speaking to one another. They would have their opportunity to play more lively tunes after the meal.

Kat and Merry arrived and were seated at the high table along with Nick.

Where was Isla? He hoped she hadn't decided to stay in her room out of anger at him. His eyes scanned the line of people entering the great hall and much to his relief he saw her. Dressed in a gown of the deepest burgundy, she seemed to float through the crowd. Gailleann wasn't with her, but he knew that she'd probably been left with one of the servants while she slept.

Aleck couldn't take his eyes off of her as she approached him. He held out a hand to her, but she ignored him and walked right past. He shook his head. His punishment for his earlier mistake. He looked up to the ceiling, cursing himself for his stupidity, before greeting the next guest.

When everyone was seated, Aleck made his way to his seat at the center of the high table. Kat was seated at his right, with Nick next to her. To his left was Isla, with Merry beside her. Before sitting, he raised his glass in a toast.

"Please raise your drinks," he said to the crowd, who all did as directed. "I'd like to make a toast to the woman for whom we've held this feast. A woman who I didnae ken existed until this past year. I raise me glass to me sister, Kat. To your life and your health."

Everyone drank and then Aleck sat.

"Thank you, Aleck. This means so much to me," Kat said.

"I wanted ye to ken that ye've been missed and I'm happy yer back where ye belong." Aleck looked at Merry, who was beaming, of course. "The person ye should be thanking is this one." He nodded his head at Merry. "She planned all of this with verra little help from me."

"Thank ye, Merry," Kat raised her glass to her.

"'Twas nary a thing. I enjoyed it." Merry shyly sipped her wine.

Aleck glanced Isla's way. He knew this wasn't going to be easy. "I'm happy ye've joined us. Are ye feeling better?"

Her eyes snapped to his face and he realized he'd said the wrong thing, yet again. "There was nae a thing wrong with me. I *was* well and I *am* well." She turned her body away from him to face Will and his wife who sat beside Merry.

"Isla, I'm sorry. I always seem to say or do the wrong thing with you. Please forgive my oafishness." He may as well have been speaking to himself. She didn't respond or even turn around. "I believe I've angered yer sister," he whispered to Merry.

"Ye have, but I'm still speaking to ye." Merry laid a hand on his. "Dinnae fear. She'll be over it soon enough and ye'll be back in her good graces."

"I ken I've told ye before, but ye are a wonder, Merry. Ye'll make some man a verra good wife."

CHAPTER 20

Pierce Holmes was feeling confident. He'd done a good job of disguising himself and staying away from Nick Mackall and Katriona. They were the only people here who could possibly recognize him as a threat. He skulked around the castle being careful to look as if he belonged in order to find out where the bairn was being kept. He heard a kitchen maid get tasked with taking a tray of food with a special plate for the baby upstairs so he followed the woman and watched to see which chamber she entered. He now felt he had a very good chance of getting to little Molly Sinclair and bringing her to the rock prison where the sword was kept.

In the meantime, he was hungry and there was a feast taking place in the great hall. He found an empty seat and sat down beside a raucous group of men whom he assumed were the Sinclair men at arms. They didn't seem to mind his company and were happy to ignore him while he scarfed down every bit of food that landed in front of him. A decent meal was hard to come by when on a mission. He'd eat and then while everyone was enjoying music and dance he'd collect Molly and be on his way. With any luck, he'd be far away from here before they knew she was missing.

"There he is again," Kat said.

"He's the man who won the race," Nick said. "He had the hood over his face most of the time, but I know it was him."

"Who is he?" Kat stared at him. "This is driving me crazy. I know

I've met him somewhere before."

"I have the same feeling. Let's think about this for a moment. We both know him, but aren't sure where we know him from. Has he been a guest at Dunnet Head?"

"Nae. I dinnae believe so."

"Then we would have met him before we knew each other, which means you either know him from the future or from the time after ye first arrived here."

"Hmmm…"

"I met ye when I was returning from the future, so it would seem that is where I ken him from."

They both thought about that and then turned to face each other.

"I know who he is," Kat said.

"As do I," Nick replied.

"His name is Pierce Holmes. He worked for Malcolm Granger. I only met him two or three times and verra briefly, but I'm sure it's him."

"Aye. I met him in San Francisco. He was one of Granger's men. His hair is a bit different and he's in need of a bath, but 'tis him."

When they looked back out at everyone enjoying their food, Holmes was gone.

"He must realize we know who he is." Nick turned to Aleck. "Where's Gailleann?"

"She's asleep in Isla's chamber."

"What's wrong," Isla joined the conversation.

"The man who won the race today. He's from the future. Kat and I just realized we know who he is."

"Do ye believe he's here for Gailleann?" Isla asked.

Nick nodded.

"Where is he?"

"He was just here. Kat and I were trying to understand where we knew him from and when we looked away to speak with each other he disappeared."

Aleck shot up from his chair, followed by Isla. "Stay here with

149

our guests. I'll take care of this."

"I'm coming with ye," Isla said.

There was no time to argue. He bolted from the room with Isla right behind. They headed straight up to her chamber. The door stood wide open, spilling light into the passageway. Aleck put a finger to his lips and they both hugged the wall as they made their way to the door. Someone was whimpering. Aleck peeked in and then ran straight into the room. Isla joined him. Pierce was gone and so was Gailleann. The only one in the room was the servant who'd been charged with watching her. She was crumpled into a ball on the floor, holding her face and crying.

Aleck lifted her up and sat her on the edge of the bed. "Where did they go?"

"I dinnae ken, sir. He knocked me to the floor and I was too frightened to look."

"Come, Isla."

She grabbed her sword and scabbard from the chamber and followed him as he ran down the hall. "He'll need his horse if he's to make his escape."

They ran for the stables. By now, Nick was running right alongside them. "Did he take her?"

"Aye," Isla answered.

"He won't get far," Aleck said.

"How do we know his horse was in the stable?" Isla asked.

"We don't, but we'll need our horses to go after him."

They hit the stable running full speed. The doors flew open startling the sleeping stable boys who told them Pierce hadn't been there. They quickly grabbed and saddled their horses. Nick ordered the stable boys to head into the great hall to quietly retrieve his men without disrupting the feast. "Tell them to get their horses and to follow after us."

"Aye, sir." They ran to do his bidding.

They had no idea where Pierce would have gone with Gailleann, but there was no time to waste.

While Isla helped one of the lads get her horse saddled and ready to go, Aleck was busy shouting commands to his men. He turned back to see Isla mounted and kicking her horse into a full gallop. She flew past him. Aleck vaulted onto Brychan and gave chase. "I'll go with Isla," he shouted to Nick, who had slowed to direct his men.

Aleck checked back over his shoulder and saw Nick peel off in the opposite direction followed by about half of his men. The others took off down the path towards the stream. Aleck's teulu headed his way. He knew Pierce didn't have much of a head start on them. Riding at the pace they were, he felt sure they'd come upon him shortly, but then he remembered the speed of the man's horse and the lack of control Pierce had exhibited over him. How could he possibly hope to ride like that with a bairn? This worried him more than anything. They had to get to Gailleann before she was killed.

THE ONLY THING on Isla's mind was getting to Gailleann. If that man caused her any harm, he'd pay for it with his life. She was so worried that it was almost crippling her, but she wouldn't allow it. She focused her mind on rescuing Gailleann and put all other thoughts out of her head. It was the only way she was going to be able to do this. She knew Aleck and his men were behind her and she was grateful for it. She also knew that she didn't really need them. She was perfectly capable of fighting this foe on her own.

The night sky burst to life with thousands of stars and a bright moon, a blessing to be sure. They continued riding, unsure if they'd taken the wrong track and perhaps one of the other groups out searching had found Gailleann. Isla wondered if they should perhaps turn around and head back. She slowed her horse to a trot and then a walk.

Aleck rode up beside her. "Do ye see something?" he asked.

"Nae. I wonder if Nick or one of the other's found them."

"They would send a messenger with word."

"What if he never left the castle? What if we've been chasing a ghost?"

"I hadn't thought of that, but it doesnae seem likely that he'd hide there instead of making a run for it."

"Something is telling me to turn back," Isla said.

"Are ye sure?"

"Aye. We'll go slow. Mayhap we'll see something that will guide us."

"As ye wish," Aleck said.

Isla was pleased that he hadn't argued with her. She expected he might, but he seemed fine letting her lead the way.

"We're turning back," he said to the men. "Keep yer eyes open as we ride in case we missed something along the way.

The men fell in place behind them. As they went, they searched a little further off the path, following any sounds that came to their ears. None of it revealed the whereabouts of Pierce Holmes or Gailleann.

They all met again at the gates of the castle.

"Did ye see anything at all?" Isla asked.

"Nae a thing," Nick answered.

"I should have had the men search the castle grounds, but I was sure he'd want to be on his way in a hurry," Aleck said.

As they entered the courtyard, Merry came running. "Nick, he's got Kat." She pointed to the postern gate.

Nick kicked his horse into a gallop and rounded the castle before the others even moved. Aleck and Isla were next to follow and then the others came up behind. As they approached the postern gate, they could all see a terrified Kat, standing next to Pierce and Gailleann who were both astride the prancing black stallion who seemed ready to bolt. Holmes seemed to have his hands full holding Gailleann and keeping the horse from running away with them. Kat stood completely still, a rope around her neck was attached to the saddle. Aleck's heart was in his throat.

"Holmes, let Kat go," Nick said.

"She's my security," he answered.

"What do ye want for her release and the release of the bairn?" Aleck asked.

Holmes laughed, "Nothing you can give me!"

"No money or jewels could change yer mind?"

"I'm here for the sword!" he shouted. "Once I have it, I'll have all the money, jewels and power one man could want." Little Gailleann was crying in his arms. Aleck willed her to be still so she wouldn't fall.

"Ye ken ye willnae get it. Too many are working to keep ye from it."

"Who? Is it that witch Edna?" He glared warily at them.

Aleck didn't have an answer to that question, but he thought if the witch frightened him then he'd go along with it. "Aye. And the elves and faeries as well."

"Pierce, please, let me go. You have to know that Ariweth, the sorcerer, is probably the one who drew you here. It's what happened last time you were here with Malcolm." Kat's face was as white as the moon above. Her eyes were on Nick, pleading for his help.

"Aye." Nick said. "Malcolm ended up dead and the same fate could befall ye if ye dinnae forget about the sword."

"I'll nae forget about it!" he screamed at them. "'Tis why I'm here. I havenae come this far to give up." His horse jumped and Kat's hands flew to her throat, holding onto the rope as it tightened and pulled her feet from the ground.

The crowd around him gasped, then out of nowhere, Isla was beside them. She sliced the rope that held Kat and tried to grab Gailleann. Pierce evaded her and let his horse fly out the gate and across the field. The riders all fell in line behind Isla who was determined to catch him.

HORSES STREAKED ACROSS the field as Aleck did his best to catch up with Isla. His first thought when he saw her race through the gate was that she would fall and be hurt, but now he had to admit he admired her abilities atop the horse. She hugged with her legs and crouched low over the horse's neck. She was so close to Holmes, she'd be on him in a matter of moments. Aleck kicked his horse up to his fastest speed. He had to get there before Isla did something crazy. He rode up along the other side of Holmes, but his horse was a natural born racer. Catching sight of Isla and Aleck the horse lunged forward with Holmes hanging on for dear life. Thankfully he had a death grip on Gailleann, who was shrieking.

"Dinnae be afraid, my love," Isla called over the pounding hoofbeats. "I'll save ye!"

Holmes looked back and as he did he lost his balance and yanked the reins back to reseat himself. His horse crow-hopped, tossing his head, fighting to unseat his rider, finally tossing Pierce and Gailleann into the air. In a split second, Isla positioned herself in such a way that the bairn miraculously landed in her arms. She continued to charge forward. Aleck leaped from Brychan and was preparing to do battle with Holmes, when he noted that he was already back atop his horse and charging after Isla. A green light in the distance beckoned to them and Aleck knew Anania was waiting.

"Run, Isla! He's right behind ye. Run to the green light!"

He hopped atop his steed once again and gave chase. He was too far behind now but still, he continued on. His men followed him. As he got closer, he could see Anania speaking with Isla. Holmes and the horse appeared to be paralyzed, unable to move. That's when Aleck realized he was not getting any closer to Isla. His horse and his men were all frozen in place.

"I'LL TAKE THE bairn now, Isla. Thank ye for keeping her safe these past days," Anania said, holding out her arms.

"Nae. I cannae give her to you." Isla shielded Gailleann with her body.

"Ye must. She will return to her family in the future," Anania moved closer.

"I'm going with her." Isla backed away.

Gailleann's eyes were open wide as she looked at Anania. "Mama?" she asked.

Anania tipped her head to the side, raising an eyebrow and tapping her dainty foot. "She must leave now. I can only hold them for a little while longer."

"I'm going with her. I must be sure she is safe."

Anania seemed to give it some thought and then the green light swallowed them all and they were gone.

ALECK COULDN'T BELIEVE his eyes. "Isla, nae!" he yelled. He ran into the middle of what had just a moment ago been a circle of green light, but Isla, Gailleann and Anania were gone.

Aleck turned to Pierce Holmes, but he was gone as well and he'd taken his horse with him. Had he merely ridden away or had he gone to the future? None of his men saw what had happened. They all had their eyes fixed on the green light.

"Damn it all!" Aleck roared. He stood there not knowing what to do. This was not something he had much experience with. Aleck was always decisive in everything he did. His men sat quietly atop their horses waiting for him to say something.

"Aleck!" Nick rode up behind them. "Where are they?"

"They're gone."

"Gone? Where?"

"I can only assume to the future where wee Gailleann is from."

He dismounted and stood beside Aleck. Neither man spoke.

Aleck's eyes searched the area, expecting to see Isla somewhere out there, but it was clear she was gone. "Will she come back?" he asked.

"I did. Kat did, but it took a long time for both."

Aleck felt like a spear went through his heart. "Are ye telling me I'll never see her again?"

"Nae. Of course, ye will. We'll find a way to contact Anania or better still, Edna Campbell. She can help."

"How do ye ken it?"

"She brought me back and I have a feeling she can return Isla."

"Where is she?"

"She's in the future but, if I remember correctly, ye can speak with her through the hearth."

Aleck thought Nick must have lost his mind. "Yer daft."

"I may well be, but not about that. Come. Let's give it a try. If I'm right, I believe she kens exactly what's been happening here."

CHAPTER 21

I SLA THOUGHT SHE must be dreaming when the green glow faded and she found herself in an unusual shop with the most delicious aroma. The floors were filled with black and white tiles and an expanse of glass covered dozens of baked goods. Light shone down from glass globes hanging from the ceiling. An older woman stood staring at her as if she were seeing a ghost.

"Who are ye?" she asked.

"I be Isla," she answered.

"Is that Molly ye've got in yer arms?" The woman came out from behind the glass expanse and held her arms out to wee Gailleann.

"I call her Gailleann," Isla said, holding the bairn a wee bit tighter.

"Maureen!" the woman yelled. "Maureen!"

She ran to a side door and opened it, crying out once again. "Maureen!"

"I'm coming! I'll be right there." a woman's voice came from up above.

"Now, Maureen! Hurry!"

The sound of someone running down a flight of stairs came from the doorway and a young woman of about her own age, burst through the door and immediately began to cry.

"Mama!" Gailleann cried. She squirmed in Isla's arms and held her arms out to the woman.

"Molly!" Maureen held her arms out for her daughter.

Isla hesitated, not wanting to give her up, but realized it was the right thing to do. As much as she'd grown to love her. This wee Molly wasnae her daughter. She handed her to Maureen, who wrapped her arms around her and buried her face in the crook of the child's neck.

"Thank ye for bringing her back," she said, when she finally lifted her head.

Isla thought her heart might beat right out of her chest when she first arrived, but when she saw mother and child reunited, all the apprehension she'd felt about this moment flew away. The mixture of emotion she saw on Maureen's face soothed and wiped away Isla's concern for wee Gailleann. She wished to hold the child in her arms once again, missing the warmth and love the little one had provided her over the past weeks, but she knew she would have to find her own warmth now. Gailleann was right where she belonged and Isla was proud of herself. She'd done the one thing she hadn't wanted to do and the result of her good deed was a clarity about her own life and her own path.

Molly was trying to wipe the tears from her mother's face. "Yer Da is going to be so happy to see ye, love."

"Where is David?" Mrs. May asked.

"He's with Dylan and Maggie. They're trying to speak with Edna. They are at the hotel across the street. Please, will ye go fetch him for me."

"Of course," Mrs May replied. "I'll be right back." She hurried through the bakery door and Isla watched through the window as she ran across the road and disappeared from sight.

Maureen sat down with little Molly on her lap and motioned for Isla to sit.

Tears dropped from Isla's eyes as she sat opposite the happy mother and child. She reached out a trembling hand and placed it on Molly's back. "I'll miss ye, Gailleann," she said.

"Who's Gailleann?" Maureen asked.

"'Tis what I called her. We found her in a rainstorm and didnae ken her name." She stared at mother and daughter with a longing she'd never experienced. She wished to be a mother. She wanted

158

to have children of her own. It had been wrong to want to keep this child. It was clear to her now, but in order to do that she needed to go home. Panic began to set in. "How will I get back? I cannae stay here."

"Don't worry. We'll figure it out, but in the meantime, ye can stay with us," Maureen said.

"Thank ye." She was grateful to have shelter with this woman and Molly, but she wanted to go home.

"Is the man gone?" Maureen asked.

Isla must have looked confused.

"The man who wanted to hurt her."

"I'm nae sure. I think he's still in my time," Isla answered.

"How will we keep him from coming back for Molly?"

"Aleck and Nick will see to him. He'll nae bother ye again," she assured Maureen.

"Who are Aleck and Nick?" she asked.

"Aleck Sinclair and Nick Mackall. 'Twas Aleck who was with me when we found Gailleann. I'm sorry… Molly."

"It's okay. I understand it's what ye've been calling her. What year did ye travel from?"

"1517," Isla said. "What year is this?"

"2017. Five hundred years in the future. This must be terribly overwhelming for ye. Did Molly get to meet her many times great grandfather?"

Isla had no idea what she meant and it showed.

"Aleck Sinclair," Maureen said. "My husband is a direct descendant."

"Aleck?" Isla perked up at the mention of his name. "He's Gailleann's… I'm sorry, Molly's relative?"

"Aye. Dylan, my husband's cousin brought the family tree. It goes back hundreds of years and shows they are both descendants of Aleck Sinclair."

"Oh, my." Isla couldn't believe it. Do ye ken who their grandmother is?"

"Ye mean Aleck's wife?"

"Aye."

"I don't recall, but I'm sure her name is on the tree. They'll be back shortly and ye can see for yerself."

Molly was tucked against her mother's chest, holding her shirt just as she'd done with Isla. Maureen held her as if she were afraid she might disappear again. It was a tender moment for mother and child. Isla needed to touch that soft wee cheek and so reached out her hand, gently rubbing it. Molly placed her hand atop Isla's and whispered, "Isla."

"Thank ye again for taking care of her. I can see ye've developed a bond with her."

"She is a pleasure. Ye are lucky to have her." She meant it.

The door opened and David Sinclair entered, followed by Maggie and Dylan. He saw Molly and fell to his knees in front of her. "My precious girl!" He scooped her from her mother's lap and hugged her tightly.

"Da," Molly cooed.

Isla could feel the tears sliding down her face. The love this father had for his daughter was so beautiful.

"This is Isla," She heard Maureen introducing her to the others and tore her eyes away from the man.

"Isla Sinclair?" Dylan asked.

She was surprised by this, and corrected him, "Isla Mackall."

"Right. Yer name was Mackall before ye married Aleck."

Isla went very still. If she were to marry Aleck then these would be her descendants, too. "I am to marry Aleck?" she asked.

"Ye mean yer not married yet?"

"Nae," She whispered

Dylan smiled at her. If she looked closely, she saw a bit of Aleck in his eyes. "But if ye don't, then we won't exist."

She shook her head. Could she believe what she was hearing. This was all too much for her. "How do ye know this?"

"Here, I'll show you." Dylan pulled out a flat silver object that he opened. His fingers tapped away at black buttons and an image appeared before her very eyes. "This is my family tree. Do ye see here, it says Aleck Sinclair and Isla Sinclair?"

She couldn't believe her eyes. It did say her name, but then again maybe it was another Isla. She looked up to find them all staring at her with strange expressions on their faces. "Is something wrong?"

They all shook their heads. Dylan stood and went to her, he hugged her. "I'm so happy to meet you. I would never have thought this was possible."

David followed him. They were treating her as if she were a queen. There was a warmth and reverence they were expressing to her and she couldn't help but be drawn in by it. If they were correct, she would have children and the Sinclair line would carry on for generations right down to little Molly. "If what ye say is true, I must get back to Aleck."

"Yes. You're right. I'll contact Edna. She can take care of it. Although I'd like to meet Aleck."

"Can Anania bring him?" David asked.

"Let's find out." Dylan said.

CHAPTER 22

A s they rode into the courtyard, Merry searched for Isla and Gailleann. "Where are they?" she asked.

"They're gone," Aleck said without thinking.

"Gone!" She began to cry uncontrollably.

Aleck jumped down from his horse to comfort her. "Merry, calm yerself. They've been taken to the future. To return Gailleann to her Ma and Da. Dinnae cry. She'll be back."

"But how? When?" She sniffled into her hankie.

Aleck held her close and felt that spear twist in his heart. "I dinnae have the answer to those questions," he said.

Merry stopped crying and pulled away from Aleck to speak with her brother. "Nick?"

"Aye, Merry. I've been to the future and I've come back. Kat has been to the future and she's returned as well. Dinnae fear, Isla will return."

"But when? Ye were gone for two years and Kat since she was a bairn."

"Merry, we've got to contact Edna Campbell. We're going inside to try right now."

Her brother and Aleck left her standing in the courtyard. Taegen approached her. "Lady Merry, all will be well."

Somehow when he said it, it seemed true. The strong timbre of his voice resonated deep inside her.

"I'd hate to lose her, Taegen. She's me only sister."

"She'll be back. And sooner than ye think."

"Ye seem so sure. How do ye know this?"

"I cannae say, but I dinnae wish to see ye this way. Please believe that what I've told ye is the truth." He put out his arm for her to take. "Come. I'll walk with ye to the great hall."

"Thank ye. The guests are still here. I'm afeared they will be for some time. Mayhap into the wee hours of the morning."

"'Tis possible and Sir Aleck needs ye to see that they are all well fed and happy."

He escorted her inside where he left her. He knew that if she kept busy it would give her less time to think about her sister. Once she was mingling with the guests, Taegen took his leave.

He vaulted onto his horse and rode out at a gallop to the glen where he knew he'd find Anania. The full moon cast a circle of light around her where she stood.

"Taegen, there ye be," she said.

He dismounted and went to her. "Mother," he said, bowing his head to her.

"There's nae need for ye to be so formal with me." She touched his face with her long, slender fingers. "All went as planned. The bairn is safely back with her Ma."

"When will Lady Isla return? Her sister is frantic over losing her."

"She hasnae lost her. She will return, but first Sir Aleck must go forward in time to retrieve her. Everything will become clear once that has happened. Dinnae fret over Lady Merry. She will be happy once again when her sister returns to her." Her vibrant green eyes crinkled in the corners as she smiled at her son.

Taegen knew it to be true, but still he hated to see Lady Merry so sad. "Shall I tell Sir Aleck to return here?"

"Nae. Isla needs some time without him to realize he is the one for her. What is it they say? Absence makes the heart grow fonder?

We will let him believe that it is Edna who must help him."

"Is there anything ye need of me?"

"Aye. Find Pierce Holmes. Follow him and make sure that he has been released from Ariweth's spell."

"What if he hasnae?"

"If he remains a threat, I'm afraid ye'll have to kill him."

Taegen knew that to be true, even before she said it. "I'll see to it."

"Remember who ye are, Taegen. It is our duty to protect those who cannae protect themselves from magic and sorcery."

He bowed to his mother who shook her finger at him. "I would like a hug from my son."

Taegen wrapped his mother in a warm embrace. He loved her dearly, but he had been banished from the elven realm because his father was a human. He knew his mother would gladly have allowed him to stay, but the Council of Elders made the decision and they refused to change their minds. And so, he would live his life among mortals not really belonging with them either.

He mounted his horse knowing his inner guidance would direct him to Holmes. He hoped the man would soon be released from the spell. It wasnae his doing that he was even in this time and Taegen would prefer not to kill an innocent man. But as long as Ariweth existed, the Sinclair children would be at risk and it was Taegen's job to keep them safe. He would do whatever was necessary.

ALECK FELT LIKE a daft idjit standing in front of his hearth calling out to a woman he didn't know, who may or may not be able to help him. They'd been at this for two days and nothing had happened.

"I feel I'd have better luck locating Anania, although I don't know where I'd even begin to look," Aleck said.

"You could be right," Nick said.

The feast had continued on in the great hall without any of

the Sinclair's or Mackall's. Some had remained at the castle for a few days and while Aleck had done his best to be a good host, his mind was elsewhere. It was now well after midnight and Aleck was exhausted. "We should rest. We may need all of our energy to solve this puzzle."

"Kat's already asleep, but I would like to join her," Nick said.

"Go. We'll speak more in the morning."

Nick placed a hand on his shoulder and gave it a squeeze before leaving him alone at the hearth.

He sat back in his chair and closed his eyes, thinking of Isla and Gailleann and hoping they'd made it to their destination safely. He'd almost drifted off when the fire sparked, causing him to jump. He glanced around the room, but he was alone.

"Aleck?" a woman's voice floated through the air to his ears.

"Aye. Where are ye?" He glanced around the darkened room and then focused on the hearth.

"Ye cannae see me, but I'm Edna Campbell. I'm here to help ye. Ye should ken that Isla and the bairn are fine."

Aleck was so relieved he fell back in the chair. The uncertainty had been a heavy weight to bear and he knew, now that he could face anything that needed to be done. "When will Isla come back?" he asked. He was missing her terribly and he was worried for her safety.

"Ye'll need to go and get her, Aleck. Can ye do that?"

"Aye, but how?"

"Anania will help ye. Ye can go after ye've slept a while. She'll meet ye in the spot where ye last spoke. Do ye remember where that is?"

"Aye." He remembered it well and would have no trouble finding it. "Why does she nae bring Isla back here?"

"There's something in the future that ye must see."

"What is it?"

"Ye must go there to find out."

"A good thing I hope."

"Aye. 'Tis good. Ye'll be happy to make the journey."

"And Isla will come back with me?"

"She will. Now, go lie in yer bed for a while. Ye'll need yer rest."

The glow of the fire diminished and the flames flickered before extinguishing. Aleck rose and went up to his chamber where he slept peacefully for several hours.

NICK AND KAT were seated in the great hall enjoying their meal, as were a number of the other guests who had lingered here at Sinclair Castle, when Aleck joined them.

"How are ye this morn?" Kat asked.

"I'm feeling ready," Aleck answered.

"For what?" asked Nick.

"To travel through time. Edna spoke to me after ye left."

Kat jumped up and hugged Aleck, "She's going to help ye then?"

"She told me to seek out Anania today. She will send me to get Isla. She says there's something there I must see."

"And then ye'll be back?" Kat looked at him with concern. He knew she was worried that they could be separated by time once again.

"I believe so," he patted her arm reassuringly. Honestly, he did not know what to expect but he knew that he had to get Isla back, no matter what.

"I hope so. Yer needed around here, being that ye are the laird."

Aleck laughed. "I'll return. She told me I would." He stretched and loosened his neck, trying to look and act like a man who feared nothing. "What's it like? The future."

"It's a wonderous place," Nick said. "Ye'll be amazed at the things ye will see, but if yer like me, ye'll be happy to be back in yer own time."

"What kind of things will I see?"

"I could explain them to ye, but ye need to see them with yer own eyes. 'Twill be a surprise for ye."

"Nick's right. It's impossible to explain all the many things that will be different five hundred years from now."

Aleck was filled with questions, but he realized that they were right, it would be better for him to experience it for himself. "We'll have much to speak of when I return with Isla."

"Dinnae be afraid, my friend," Nick said.

"I'm nae afraid," Aleck insisted. He was fearless in the face of battle, but he had to admit to a bit of apprehension in this instance. He would never share that with Nick though. The two shared a strong competitive nature and were always trying to outdo each other. He couldn't possibly let him know. Nick would never let him live it down.

Aleck quickly broke his fast and then stood to leave.

"Do ye wish me to go with ye. I'll take yer horse back once ye've gone," Nick offered.

"I cannae take me horse with me?"

"I dinnae believe ye'd wish to or need to."

Aleck wondered why, but didn't ask. He'd find out soon enough. "Come with me then."

The two men said their goodbyes to Kat.

"I'll be back soon," Nick said.

"And I'll be back, but nae so soon," Aleck chuckled.

"Take care brother. We'll be awaiting yer return," Kat said.

EDINBURGH - 2017

IT HAD BEEN two full days since Isla was transported to this future time. In that time, she'd gotten to know the Sinclair family rather well. She'd enjoyed spending time with all of them. They were kind and caring people and it showed in so many ways. Maggie and

Dylan told her they were only visiting Edinburgh and thought it would be great fun if they all went sightseeing together. Maggie gave her some modern day clothes to wear and Isla had to admit she enjoyed wearing "jeans" as Maggie had called them. There were so many strange and wonderful things to see she thought her eyes may pop right out of her head, but they didn't. In her own time, she'd only been to Edinburgh once with her Ma and she remembered it to be filled with people, horses and carts. This Edinburgh was so different. The castle was the same and there were still so many people, but they were traveling in carriages that moved without the aid of horses. The lights she saw everywhere, lit up the night and only required the flick of a switch to illuminate entire buildings. It was all fascinating to her, but it also made her a bit anxious. The constant sounds, both pleasant and unpleasant rang in her ears both day and night. She missed the quiet of Dunnet Head and Castle Sinclair.

Today they were all going to eat at an Indian restaurant. Isla had no idea what that meant, but so far she'd been enjoying the food she'd tried. Again, it was nothing like what she had back home. Mrs. May's scones were probably the closest to anything she recognized.

"Are you ready, Gran?" Dylan asked with a chuckle.

"Why do ye call me Gran?" Isla asked. "And why do ye laugh?"

"I call you Gran because you are my many times great grandmother and I'm laughing because you don't look anything like a grandma. It's kind of funny, don't you think?"

Isla smiled warmly at Dylan. He was a good man. He'd done so much to make her feel at ease here in this strange place. "Yer right. 'Tis funny," she laughed.

He put an arm around her shoulders and escorted her out the door where the others all waited. This was her family. How lucky she was to get a glimpse into the future and to meet these wonderful people. It made her proud to think she had something to do with their lives.

At the restaurant, they sat at a large table. Maureen put Molly in a highchair next to Isla. "This will be a first for both of you," Maureen said. "Molly's never had Indian food before either."

When the food arrived at the table, the aroma of spices wafted to Isla's nose. Her curiosity took over and she examined every dish set in front of them. So many different textures, colors and sauces and nothing familiar, except of course, the bread, which was delicious. She tasted a bit of it all, but concluded that it was too spicy for her taste. Little Molly seemed to agree.

"Isla we got you a room at our hotel for tonight. I know it's been cramped for you sleeping in the apartment." Maggie locked arms with her as they made their way across a particularly busy street.

"Thank ye, Maggie." She would be excited to sleep at the hotel. It would be good to give the little family their privacy.

"Dylan and I will be right next door, so if ye need anything at all, come knock on our door. Okay?"

"Aye." Isla replied, but she was more interested in the shop windows they passed.

"Would ye like to go in?" Maggie asked.

"Can we?"

"Of course." She turned to Dylan and the others. "Isla and I are going to go shopping. You're welcome to join us, or we'll see you back at the bakery."

"I vote for the bakery," Dylan said, elbowing David.

"Agreed," David chimed in.

"Molly and I will join ye," Maureen said. "'Tis never to early to teach a wee lass the fine art of shopping."

"That's what I was afraid of," David replied, rolling his eyes skyward. "Okay. We'll see you later." He and Dylan walked off down the street and Isla noted the way the other women watched them as they walked away.

"Ye love them much, dinnae ye?" she said.

Maggie and Maureen both glanced at each other and smiled.

"We do," Maggie said. "Let's go in this store."

The women entered the shop and Isla couldn't believe all of the wonderful things she was seeing. So many clothes, all hanging on racks and laid out on tables. There were shoes on a side wall and jewelry hanging everywhere. Of course, they weren't anything Isla would wear back home, but she loved examining them and seeing how they were sewn, the fabrics they were made of and all of the unbelievable colors. She felt everything she passed. Maggie sprayed something in the air and Isla loved the scent.

"Here, try some on," Maggie said, spritzing her with a little on her wrist.

"I love it," Isla said. She knew she'd be continually putting her wrist to her nose the rest of the day. "I wish I could take some home with me."

"You can." Maggie grabbed a box and brought it to the woman who must own the shop. Isla watched with fascination as the transaction took place. No silver changed hands. Maggie used a flat object, which she took from her purse to pay. She handed Isla the bag, kissing her cheek as she did.

"Thank you," Isla said, feeling much warmth for these two women.

"It's my way of thanking you. Without you, I wouldn't have Dylan."

"And I wouldn't have David."

Isla tipped her head, thinking. "I hadn't thought of it, but yer right." A sense of pride enveloped her as they left the store and headed back to the bakery. With that thought in mind, Isla relaxed. Aleck would be here with her soon. He would meet these handsome young men and then they'd return home. She still wasn't sure she could believe she was the Isla mentioned in the tree Dylan kept. She started imagining what her life would be like as Lady Sinclair. She had to admit that her feelings for Aleck had been growing stronger with each passing day, if it hadn't been for his behavior at the mock battle, she might even say she was falling in love with him. He hadn't really done anything too terribly wrong and he was right, she could have been injured. She wondered if she could convince him of how important it was to her to continue practicing with the men. If he wouldnae, then she would have nae choice but to return to Dunnet Head and forget about him. That would be the proof she needed that she was nae the Isla he would spend his days with. He respected her in every other way and he'd been more than patient with her grumpiness and bad temper. Any man who could deal with that was a man worth having. She smiled. A sense of peace settling in. She could be Lady Sinclair and still be Isla. She didn't have to do it better than any lady of the castle ever had. She could do it her way. She already found that despite her initial protests, she could be a mother. She could nurture and raise a good, strong family.

The only thing to do now was to wait for Aleck. She hoped he hadn't changed his mind about her.

CHAPTER 23

ALECK ARRIVED AT the designated spot and found he and Nick were alone. Nick appeared a bit restless.

"What's wrong?" Aleck asked.

"I dinnae wish to travel with ye."

"I dinnae believe ye will."

"When I traveled to the future, I wasnae meant to, but I found myself in San Francisco. I'm happy here. I dinnae wish to leave again."

"Stay far back from me then." Aleck hopped off of his horse and handed the reins to Nick. "Ye can head back if ye wish. She'll be here soon."

"I believe I will. Take care. We'll see ye soon, I hope." Nick looked very serious, but then Aleck caught the gleam in his eye.

"Nick, if yer trying to frighten me, it willnae work."

Nick chuckled. "I'll be on me way then."

Aleck waved to him as he rode off then turned to wait for Anania. It was a beautiful, clear day and he could see quite a distance in every direction. He wondered how long it would be before she arrived to send him on his way. He needn't have worried, because from the corner of his eye he noticed the green glow he was now familiar with. Anania appeared beside him.

"Are ye ready, Aleck Sinclair?"

"I am."

"Then come within the circle of green and we'll be on our way."

"Are ye joining me?"

"Only to get ye there. Then I'll be gone."

"And how will we return?"

"Dinnae fear. I'll be there for ye when ye wish to come back."

He took a deep breath and stepped within the green.

Aniana began walking so Aleck fell into step beside her. "Ye spoke with Edna?"

"Aye."

"We are good friends. I have helped her many times, and she me. 'Tis important that we dinnae allow the Twin Sword to fall into the wrong hands."

"Where is Holmes?"

"He is still in yer time. Once Ariweth understands that he has failed his mission, he will release him from the spell he conjured to get him here."

"So he's been under a spell. He didnae really wish to harm Gailleann."

"That is the way of it. If Ariweth could manage it he would destroy both Edna and me, but his powers are nae so great to fight a witch and the Elven Queen."

"But I thought Holmes wanted the sword."

"He thought he did as well, but it was Ariweth, just as it was with Malcolm Granger. Ariweth willnae give up. He will continue to seek help from men he is able to control and so the Sinclair's and the Mackall's will need to be vigilant and watch for any signs that he has found his man."

"I don't understand what he wanted with Gailleann."

"It is said that the blood of a Sinclair daughter must be extracted to open the stone prison Ariweth finds himself in and to bring him back to his greatest strength."

"But why did it have to be Gailleann?"

"She was the one that was easiest for our Sir Holmes to get to. Any Sinclair daughter would do."

This sent a shiver through Aleck as he thought of his yet unborn children.

"Never fear, Sir Aleck. The elves of this land will help to protect yer children."

"Why can't ye simply destroy Ariweth?"

173

"'Tis a good question. One would think that would be easy to do, but as much as I can imprison him and keep his powers moderated, it is nae possible for me to rid the world of his presence."

"Is he so powerful?"

"I would have to release him in order to destroy him and if I failed, he would destroy me and all of my elves. I have not found a way to do it otherwise."

Aleck nodded his head in understanding.

"Are ye ready?" Anania asked.

They were still surrounded by the beautiful view of the hills, and Aleck wondered what would happen next.

"Let's be on our way," Aleck stated with the conviction of a man who wasn't frightened.

Anania closed the green light around them and moments later opened it again. Aleck found himself standing in a room filled with people who were staring at him. He glanced back behind him, but Anania and the green light were gone. He cleared his throat, ready to speak when a flash of color raced towards him. He found himself in the embrace of someone. He looked down at the top of this hugger's head and realized it was Isla. He quickly embraced her, holding her to him like a drowning man to a log.

"Aleck! Yer here!" she cried, tears of joy sparkling in her eyes.

"I am. And so are ye." She was more beautiful than he remembered. He bent to kiss her when he heard someone cough across the room. He looked up to see the others staring at him and wondered who these people could be. They appeared just as amazed as he, standing there in various forms of shocked expression. He didn't care. He continued holding onto the woman he was afraid he'd never see again and who was obviously quite happy to see him.

She pulled just far enough away to gaze up into his eyes. She seemed different to him. More at peace. The stress she always carried with her seemed to be gone. He took in the rest of her and realized she was wearing clothing the likes of which he'd never seen before. She wore some strange trews which hugged every curve of her womanly body. He was shocked at first, but had to admit he liked it.

"Aleck, come meet everyone," she took his hand and led him closer to those gaping at him. "This is Dylan." she said.

"I'm pleased to meet you," Dylan said, holding out his hand for Aleck to take.

"And I ye," Aleck shook his hand, tipping his head and gazing into his face. Something familiar there.

"This is my wife, Maggie." Dylan drew Maggie up next to him. She was a beautiful red-haired lass.

"Maggie," Aleck said, nodding his head.

"I'm Edna Campbell's niece. I believe ye ken who she is," Maggie smiled at him.

Surprise and delight lit his face. "I do. I havenae seen her face, but I've spoken with her," he smiled warmly at Maggie.

"This is David," Isla said.

"David, 'tis good to meet ye," Aleck shook hands with him, noting a resemblance between he and Dylan. He thought they might be brothers.

"I can't believe this," David said.

"Nor can I," Aleck truthfully replied.

"This is Maureen," David said, "and our wee Molly."

It took him only a moment, but when Gailleann lifted her arms to him, he knew who it was. "May I?" he asked.

"Of course," Maureen said.

He took the bairn and held her on his arm. "So, yer name is Molly," he said, gently smoothing her hair and taking a good, long look at her.

"Aw weck," she said, touching her finger to his chest.

"She remembered me name," he said, laughing.

"Why would she nae remember yer name? She's known it all along. She's been saying it since we arrived here," Isla explained. "I believe she wondered where ye were."

He was introduced to an older couple, too, and was told they owned the bakery he found himself in.

"I thought it smelled quite sweet in here," he said.

"Thank ye," Mrs. May replied. "Shall we all sit and have some tea and sweets?"

They put three of the tables together. Maureen and Isla went to help Mrs. May and the others sat down with Aleck, who was still holding Molly. He sat her on his lap and she pounded on the table.

"Alright, love, Ma will get ye something to eat," David said.

Aleck glanced around the room. It was like nothing he'd ever seen before. Tables and chairs everywhere, but not as intricately carved and fine as those of his castle. These people of the future were different. It wasn't just their clothing. Everything about them seemed unusual. They way they spoke, dressed and behaved were all of great interest to him. He wondered if seeing all of this was the reason for his journey or perhaps it was these people he'd had to meet. "I've been told I had to come here for a purpose," Aleck said. "Are all of ye the reason I'm here?"

"Could be," Dylan answered.

The women returned with trays of tea and many other delicious looking treats, placing them on the table in front of them. Everyone helped themselves. Isla placed a cup of tea and a scone in front of Aleck, who was still having a hard time believing he'd traveled through time. Isla on the other hand seemed quite at home.

"When I first arrived, I was a bit like ye. Maggie said I looked like…" she wrinkled her nose, "what did ye call it?" she asked.

"A deer in the headlights," Maggie said.

"I dinnae ken what that means, but I'm guessing 'tis how ye look right now," Isla laughed.

It was a sweet sound to his ears. "So, will ye please tell me why I'm here."

"Yer here to meet the future of the Sinclair clan," Maggie explained. "Dylan and David and wee Molly are direct descendants of your line."

Aleck looked at the two young men, neither much younger than he and took a moment to study their features.

The oddity of this situation wasn't lost on any of them. He could read it in their expressions. "To see into the future five hundred years is amazing, but to ken my family will continue on even further is even more unbelievable."

"Well, ye can believe it, because 'tis true, Maggie said.

"Tell me all about yerselves," Aleck said.

DYLAN AND DAVID were happy to fill him in on their lives and the lives of their parents. They spoke for hours, refilling tea cups and eating everything set before them. Isla held tight to Aleck's hand much of the time. She didn't wish to tell him she was the many times great-grandmother of this bunch. She was still unsure how that would all work out. Should she put her faith in a *family tree* as Dylan had called it?

"I'm going to bring Molly upstairs for a nap," Maureen said.

"Come on, Isla. We'll get you all checked in while Aleck talks with the guys."

She felt like a fish out of water. She knew she was still in Scotland. In Edinburgh, in fact. Even still, there were so many things that made no sense to her, including the way that people spoke.

"We'll be back," Maggie said. "Or maybe you could meet us at the hotel. I got them a room next to ours."

"Okay. See you in a bit," Dylan said. He'd pulled out his computer to show Aleck the family tree.

Isla turned to Maggie as they walked out the door. "Mayhap I should have me own room. Aleck and I arenae married, ye ken." She could feel the heat in her cheeks as she spoke.

"I know that and you know that, but it's not a problem in this time. Besides, do you really want to stay in a room all alone tonight? I mean, if ye do that's not a problem."

Isla gave that some thought as they crossed the street and entered another larger structure. It looked a bit like a castle from the outside, but once they entered, she stood with her mouth agape at all the wonders before her. The furnishings, rugs and marble floors were quite impressive. The laird who lived here must be very wealthy. Fascinated by the overhead lights, she almost tripped over Maggie who'd stopped in front of a large wooden desk to speak with a woman. Isla paid no attention to what they were saying. She was more interested is watching all the people who came and went. Even though she'd already been here for a few days, she still wasn't used to the sights the sounds and the large number of people she saw everywhere she went.

Maggie finished her business with the woman at the desk. "I'm a people watcher, too. I could sit on a bench all day watching the people walking by."

"I've nae seen so many people… everywhere."

"Aren't there lots of people in your clan?"

"Aye, but I know them all. 'Tis nae like this. I know nary a one of these people."

"I hadn't thought of that. It must be overwhelming for you."

"What is overwhelming?"

"More than you can handle," Maggie explained.

"Oh, nay. I wouldnae say that. I'm enjoying meself." Isla peeked back over her shoulder towards the entrance. She worried that Aleck may be feeling *overwhelmed.*

CHAPTER 24

"I can't believe what yer showing me." Aleck was delighted, of course, but unsure it could be true. "Ye mean to tell me that Isla is to be me wife?"

Dylan laughed, obviously amused at the shocked expression he wore. "She is. It says so right here. Don't you want to marry her?"

"Aye. I'm nae sure she wishes to marry."

"She seems really into you," Dylan said. "She was excited to see you," Dylan said, looking to David for help.

"The way she sat with you holding your hand, I would have thought you two were already married," David said. "Couldn't her family just order her to marry you? I thought I read somewhere that people in your time married whoever was chosen for them?"

"Not always, and not in my case. I've chosen Isla, but she hasnae yet chosen me."

"So, she doesn't like you then?" Dylan said, appearing confused.

"I think she may, but she fights it. She fights with me."

"That's nae good. Maybe we can help," David said.

"What are you fighting about?" Dylan asked.

"I've always been verra comfortable with the lasses, ye ken. Isla is different. I am oafish with her. I say daft things that upset her."

"Such as?"

"Once I told her she should smile more because she's pretty when she smiles."

"Oh, man! That's a bad one."

"How bad?"

"Not terrible, but not something you should say either."

"Anything else?"

"Aye. She was angry with me when I wouldnae allow her to take part in a swordsmanship competition. I feared she would be injured."

"Does she know how to use a sword?" David asked.

"Aye."

"Then let her, and be careful with your words."

"This is so weird. We're giving our great, great, great, great, great grandfather dating advice," Dylan shook his head and laughed.

David chuckled. "Yer right. 'Tis verra strange."

"Dating advice?" Aleck was confused.

"Do you want to take this one, David?" Dylan asked.

"Sure. Ye see, Grandda Aleck, before ye marry a woman in this time, ye date her. Ye take her out to eat, to the movies, for walks in the park. That's how ye find out if she's the one."

"Oh, I see. We do the same, I believe."

Dylan stood and stretched. "I guess you'll have to watch what you say. I can tell you that Maggie wouldn't be very happy with me if I said I wasn't going to *allow* her to do something."

"Does she nae ask yer permission?"

"No way. She's her own woman. I never tell her what to do. I might tell her that I think something is a bad idea, but ultimately, it's up to her."

Aleck nodded his understanding.

"Maggie and I will help you as much as we can, but it's going to be up to you to convince her." Dylan put his computer away. "We'll see you tomorrow, David. Let's go, Grandda." Dylan laughed and threw his arm over Aleck's shoulders. They were about the same height and physical build. It was definitely possible that people might mistake them for brothers.

Dylan was more than amused by this set of circumstances. Aleck had to stop and touch the taxicabs outside of the hotel, and then the revolving doors caught his eye. He stood and watched as people came and went through them.

"Come on," Dylan said. "Give them a try."

He waited for the door to come around and then he shoved Aleck in and followed in the next opening. He exited only to find that Aleck was still going around and around. As he approached the interior of the hotel once again, Dylan reached in and grabbed him.

"Couldn't figure out how to get out of there, huh?" Dylan observed.

"Of course not. I was merely seeing how they were constructed. I think I would like to add them to Sinclair Castle."

"Believe me, it wouldn't be a good idea," Dylan guided him to the elevators where he explained what they were and how they worked. The doors slid open as Dylan said they would. The two men entered a small room without windows and the doors closed behind them. Even though Dylan explained it all to him, Aleck was still uncertain what was about to happen. He watched as Dylan pushed a button that then lit up. The room began to vibrate, putting Aleck on edge.

"Are there nae stairs then?" Aleck asked.

"Sure. It's just easier and faster to take the elevator." The doors opened on their floor and they stepped out.

"'Tis magic," Aleck declared seeing that they were now in a totally different place.

"Not really, but I can see why you might think so," Dylan said.

Aleck followed Dylan to his room where Maggie and Isla were waiting for them.

"Did you get them a room?" Dylan asked.

"I did. Right down the hall. Isla wanted to wait for Aleck to get here."

Dylan noticed Isla's face light up when Aleck walked in the room and he winked at Maggie, who obviously had noticed as well.

"Let's show them their room," Dylan said, holding the door open.

"Can ye believe we're here, Isla?" Aleck asked.

"'Tis beyond belief," she answered.

He held his arms open and she went to him. Happiness overcame him. So much so that he began to laugh.

"Why do ye laugh?" Isla asked, lifting one eyebrow and tipping her head.

"I always thought that I knew everything about the world, but I really only knew about my life, my castle, my clan. There is so much I dinnae ken about this world. More than I can ever know."

"So yer saying yer nae so smart," Isla teased.

He laughed again. This woman he'd followed through time was what he needed in his life. She would always challenge him, speak her mind and keep him in line, without him being any less a man. The very nature of her being made him a better man.

"Isla, I wish ye to ken that from this point forward, I willnae argue with ye if ye wish to spar with the men. I ken ye understand that I love ye and I dinnae wish ye to be hurt, but I willnae try to stop ye if 'tis what ye wish."

"It is. Thank ye. I ken my stubborn ways may be vexing at times and I will do me best to listen to what ye have to say and nae be so quick to pick a fight with ye."

He lifted her chin with his hand, planting a sweet kiss on her lips. "I love ye, Isla. Will ye be me wife?"

"I will. I love ye, too." Isla pulled his head down to hers and kissed his lips, softly as first and then with a passion, matched only by his own. They sealed their vows to each other with that kiss. She would be his wife and bear their children. They would create a line that would span generations and result in David, Dylan and Molly. It was hard to fathom, but seeing it with his own eyes affirmed that what he felt for Isla was real and it would continue to grow into a partnership that would last a lifetime.

"I have something for ye. I've been carrying it with me since ye arrived at Sinclair Castle." He reached his hand inside his sporran.

"What is it?" Isla asked.

"Patience," he said. He held a small square of cloth, which he unwrapped to reveal a ring. He took her hand and placed it on her finger. It fit perfectly. Another sign, this time from the heavens. "It belonged to me Ma. She would have loved ye to wear it."

"I'd be honored." She glanced down at her finger. "'Tis beautiful."

Aleck held her hand in his, remembering his mother wearing this very same ring. The oval sapphire was set in a gold band engraved with swirls and studded with small diamonds. He had treasured this ring. The memories associated with it were warm and loving and he was happy to have Isla wear it and to continue the legacy of the Sinclair women. His lips met hers once more and lingered, kissing her again and again. He thought about how he had come so close to losing her. He would do anything at all to make her happy. He loved her strength and the fire in her eyes when they fought.

"We shall be partners in this marriage, aye?" He felt the velvety softness of her hands move under his shirt.

"I would like that verra much."

"Look at this bed, big enough for two and so inviting. Shall we make use of it?"

Though unfamiliar with the strange clothes she was wearing, Aleck quickly figured out how to get them off of her. He thought back to the one night they'd had together and wanted this night and many more to be special for her. He unbraided her hair and ran his fingers through it. He felt like the luckiest man alive. He had everything he could ever want here with this woman.

Isla climbed into the bed, watching Aleck undress. He truly was the most handsome man she'd ever met. His long blonde locks tumbled down around his broad shoulders. The muscles in his arms flexed as he removed his boots and when he stood, she admired his strong chest and narrow waist. He was hers. They'd vowed to be partners in their life together and Isla was elated by this. She wished she'd been more open to him from the start, but her stubborn ideas got in the way. Now that they were gone, she knew this was right and she felt blessed to have finally seen what was before her eyes all along.

Aleck joined her under the covers, placing a warm hand on her belly, the green of his eyes intensifying as he gazed at her. Neither of them spoke, instead enjoying the peace they'd come to know. Their lips met in soft, sweet kisses, which became more and more impassioned. Aleck pulled her beneath him as his hands explored her body, from her breasts to the apex of her thighs. He placed a knee between her legs, pushing them open and making room as he slid down her body, raining kisses across her breasts and belly as he went. Isla was in heaven. Aleck startled her when his lips and tongue delved into her womanly passage, but only for a moment before she relaxed into the incredible sensations coursing through her body. She'd never experienced anything quite so devastatingly pleasurable. She writhed in ecstasy as he continued his ministrations, sensations building more and more until she cried out as her body exploded with the intensity of her orgasm.

ALECK THRUST HIS erection into her still quivering center. He wished to give her more even while he drove himself to a fevered frenzy into her velvety warmth. Over and over again, until he didn't think he could bear it for a moment longer and then Isla cried out again, her channel spasming around his swollen cock until he joined her, spilling his seed into her womanly center.

Out of breath and completely sated, he lay back on the pillows. Isla lay nestled in the crook of his arm. He lifted his head to gaze at her. "'Twas good," he said.

"'Twas excellent," she answered.

A deep chuckle erupted from his throat. He had satisfied his woman. *His* woman. He'd thought it impossible to turn Isla's heart his way, but somehow he had. Stranger events couldn't have been more perfectly placed on their path. Perhaps it was what was needed to bring them together. He would be sure to thank Anania and let her know that he would be there for her whenever she needed his assistance. For now, he would bask in the joy he was feeling and sleep.

ISLA RESTED HER head on his chest feeling at one with this noble Highlander. All her worries were set aside here in his arms. She felt safe with Aleck. All would be well. His steady breathing as he slept lulled her to sleep, where she dreamed of a family filled with bairns and a castle filled with happiness.

CHAPTER 25

ALECK STRETCHED AND yawned before sitting up in bed. "Good morn to ye, love." He leaned over and placed a kiss on Isla's cheek.

Her eyes popped open in surprise, but then a smile appeared on her lips, "Good morn."

"Did ye sleep well?"

"Verra." She sat up, placing her hand on his back.

"We should rise," Aleck said, getting out of bed. He walked to the window where the morning had dawned and bright sunlight shined on his face. Isla joined him.

"'Tis a beautiful city," Isla noted. "Aleck?"

"Aye."

"How will we get back home?"

"Anania will help us," Aleck assured her.

"But how will we find her? What if we cannae find her?" There was a note of panic in her voice.

He pulled her close where she rested her head on his chest. "Isla I'm happy to be with ye, no matter where we find ourselves." He felt her relax in his arms. "She'll come for us. Dinnae fear."

"I wish I was as sure as ye," she said.

"She told me she would and I believe her. Have ye nae enjoyed it here?"

"Aye. I've enjoyed meeting our family, but 'tis nae our home. I want to go home."

From their window, they could see the city streets stretching out before them for miles. The roads were filled with people already out and about. A car horn honked, directing Aleck's gaze towards the park. "Did ye see that?" he asked, pointing in the direction of the park.

"What are ye looking at?"

"The park. Over there. There it is again." There was a very distinct green glow among the trees that seemed to be moving through the park.

"Is it her? Is she here?"

"Shall we go for a walk and see?" They hurried to get dressed. Isla put on her own clothes and not those Maggie had given her. She looked in the mirror, pleased with what she saw. She adjusted her gown and then turned to Aleck. "Do ye think people will stare at us. We're nae dressed as they are."

"Dinnae concern yerself with them. I dinnae care what they think. I'm with the most beautiful woman in all of Scotland and nothing they say or do will diminish the joy I feel when ye're by me side."

Isla was stunned for a moment at his words, then smiled, "Alright."

"We'll say goodbye to everyone before we go."

They gathered the few things they'd brought with them. Aleck watched as Isla put the bottle of perfume Maggie purchased her in her pocket. He smiled. There was no way she was leaving it behind.

THE SWEET SMELLS of the bakery wafted to their noses as they entered. Everyone they'd come to know during their brief stay in this time was seated and indulging in Mrs. May's delicious sweets.

"We're off for a walk to the park. We wanted to say goodbye." Aleck helped himself to a blueberry muffin from the platter on the table.

"Is Anania coming for ye?" Maggie asked.

"Today may be the day," Aleck said, smiling warmly at this lovely woman. "I'm so happy to have met ye. I'm even happier to ken that yer our family. Please give our best to Edna and thank her for her part in all of this."

"We will," Dylan said. He hugged Aleck, who held onto him for a good long time. "Yer a good lad. I'll miss ye."

"I'm so happy I've gotten to meet ye, Grandda," Dylan chuckled.

Aleck held him at arms length and memorized his face. Next he turned to David, who stood by waiting for his turn. "You, young man, have a beautiful wife and bairn. I wish ye a good life. Take care of them."

"I will," David said. He, too, received an extra long hug from Aleck.

Maureen, Maggie and Mrs. May all received hugs and kisses from Aleck and Isla, but wee Molly got more than that. Aleck twirled her around as he held her in his arms. She laughed a contagious belly laugh and all the adults in the room joined her.

Isla took her from Aleck. "Wee one, I hope ye remember me. I will remember ye. Ye be a good lass for yer Ma and Da." Tears formed in her eyes and she fought to hold them back. She hugged Molly close, not wanting her to see the tears. Maureen took her from Isla, who wiped her eyes and sniffled. "Goodbye, my wee love."

Molly waved her little hand. Isla hugged and kissed everyone again. "Goodbye. 'Tis been wonderful meeting ye all."

"Till we meet again," Maggie said.

"Do ye think we will?" she asked, hope shining in her eyes.

"One never knows. It's certainly possible."

"Oh, I hope so."

Aleck and Isla left the bakery after another round of hugs and slowly made their way to the park. They sat on a bench under a large oak tree, Isla resting her head on Aleck's shoulder. The day was beautiful. Perfect for sitting and daydreaming. They both stared up at the fluffy white clouds in the sky as they slowly floated past. People passed by them and hardly gave them any notice whatsoever. Aleck felt as if he could sit here in this spot with Isla by his side all day and he would, if need be.

A slight buzzing sound like a bee nearby broke the silence. They noted that they were alone in the park and other than the buzzing it had become very quiet.

"Look," Isla said, pointing across the park.

"'Tis the green light. Anania is here," Aleck took Isla by the hand and hurried her across the grass.

"Are ye ready to go home?" Anania asked.

"Yes," Isla cried.

They both entered the circle of green, which closed around them and before they knew what had happened they found themselves on the outskirts of Sinclair Castle.

"Anania, thank ye for allowing me a glimpse into the future. I feel that without ye, Isla and I may nae have found each other."

"I believe ye would. It may have taken ye much longer, but I was happy to be of service."

"If ye ever need me sword…" Aleck began.

"Or mine," said Isla.

"Ye'll be the first I call upon." She smiled warmly at them, waved her arm, and vanished from sight.

"We're back!" Isla shouted, jumping into Aleck's arms.

"We're home." Aleck had never been so happy to see it.

They took a moment to drink it all in before walking hand in hand towards the gates.

Scotland - 1517

"They're back," Merry cried. She'd been walking the battlements for days searching for them. She ran down the stairs and greeted them as they entered the courtyard. "You're back!" She threw herself into Isla's arms. "I've missed ye so!" She held onto Isla for dear life.

"And what of me? Did ye miss me as well?" Aleck teased.

"Aye. Of course." She went from Isla to Aleck and hugged him just as tightly.

"Have ye managed the castle in me absence?" Aleck asked.

"I have, with Nick and Kat's help. They'll be so excited yer here."

Aleck put his arm around Isla, who lifted her head to gaze up at him. Merry was pleased to see that something happened to bring them together. "Ye seem happy," she observed.

"We are," Isla said.

"We're to marry." Aleck added.

Merry shrieked with joy. "We must plan the wedding. When will it be?"

"Slow down, Merry," Isla laughed. "We'll marry as soon as we can. I'm so happy ye'll be here with us."

"We must send for Ma. She'll want to be here."

"Of course. I'll send Taegen to escort them back."

"Taegen has gone off somewhere." Merry's happy face dropped into sadness. "I dinnae ken where he is."

"How long has he been gone?" Aleck became a bit concerned.

"I havenae seen him since ye left."

"I'm sure he'll return," Aleck said. Taegen was a good fighter, he didn't need to worry about him right now.

Nick and Kat came out of the great hall to greet them.

"Yer back!" Nick said.

"So it would seem," Aleck laughed.

"I hope ye dinnae mind if I hug ye. I must be sure yer real," Nick teased.

The two men hugged and clapped each other on the back. "'Tis good to be back," Aleck said.

"Welcome home," Kat said. Hugging Isla first and then Aleck. "Things went well, I assume."

"Verra. We left wee Molly... 'tis her real name... with her Ma and Da," Aleck said.

"More importantly, we found out that Molly and her Da are Sinclair's, directly descended from Aleck," Isla proudly shared.

"Truly?" Nick said.

"Aye. We met a young man named Dylan Sinclair who is also a descendant."

"Ye must have been thrilled," Kat said.

"More than I can express. 'Tis good to know my line will continue on for hundreds of years. And that Isla is the woman I'll be spending the rest of me life with."

"I'm so happy for ye both," Kat said. "I knew you were perfect for each other." She elbowed Nick.

"I was in on that as well," he said.

"And I was too stubborn to see it," Isla said. "I wish I hadnae been so stubborn. Truth be told, I knew it as well."

Nick and Kat were beaming, as was Merry.

"We should go in. We've a wedding to plan," Isla said.

THE WEDDING WAS held as soon as Lettie Mackall and the rest of the Mackall clan arrived. Kat gifted Isla with one of the many gowns she'd purchased while she was in Edinburgh. Merry and Lettie helped tailor it so that it fit as if it were made for her.

"Thank ye so much for the beautiful gown. What made ye purchase it for me?" Isla wondered, preparing to remove the dress as the wedding wasn't until the next day.

"Wait. Let me look at ye," Kat said, circling Isla. "I had a feeling there'd be a wedding in yer future. I saw the gown and thought of ye standing by Aleck's side. That was all it took." Kat took Isla's hand, admiring the work the ladies had done. "Ye look so beautiful."

"I never even imagined myself to be beautiful, despite the fact that ye all told me often. I never even believed myself to be lovable. I believed I didn't deserved to be married and thought that, perhaps, was why Derrick was taken from me. Now, I know that those thoughts and beliefs were keeping me from being happy. Aleck saw through it all and despite it all, he loves me." She was amazed

191

and delighted by this. A few short weeks ago, she stubbornly had decided she wouldn't ever allow herself to be loved or married. She was so grateful Aleck had been patient with her.

THE EXCITEMENT FELT that day by the Mackalls and Sinclairs was expressed in beaming smiles and happy tears as Aleck and Isla spoke their vows to one another.

Two feasts in such a short time was uncommon for Sinclair Castle, but with the help of Merry, Kat and Lettie, the wedding feast was even better than Kat's celebration. The entire Sinclair clan was present, as were the local villagers, crofters and clan members from adjoining lands. The celebration lasted all day and long into the night. Merry was especially happy when Taegen returned in time for the music and dancing.

"Yer back," she observed. "Where did ye go off to?" She didn't mind that it really wasn't any of her business to ask.

"I had business to attend to," he glanced around the room until his icy blue gaze met her eyes. A smile replaced the seriousness he wore on his arrival.

"Ye disappeared and I was worried."

"I'm sorry. I didnae mean to worry anyone. Me mother summoned me to ask for help, and so I went."

Merry wanted so badly to ask what his mother needed him for, but she felt he didn't wish to share that information with her and so she remained silent.

"I'm sorry, Merry. I'm nae used to answering to anyone other than Laird Sinclair. He wasnae here and so I took my leave to attend to my mother's business."

She couldn't contain herself. "Why did she need ye?" she blurted out.

"She was concerned for a man who needed help. She couldnae

attend to it."

"And ye helped him."

"Aye. All is well with him I am happy to say." He glanced at the dance floor and then back to Merry. "Would ye care to dance?"

"I would." She happily allowed him to escort her onto the dance floor where she was surprised at what a good dancer he was.

"Taegen, there ye be," Aleck said, as they bumped into each other.

"Sir. May I congratulate ye on yer wedding."

"Ye may. I'm happy yer back."

"He was helping his mother," Merry added.

"As any good son should," Isla added.

"I hope ye werenae worried I wouldnae return," Taegen said.

"Nae. I ken ye are a devoted captain to me men. Ye wouldnae leave without reason."

They continued on their way. Taegen smiled down at Merry, who returned his smile.

"Ye are a good friend to have worried about me," he said.

"Ye were a good friend to help me with Aleck and Isla," she said, laughing as he twirled her around and around.

Isla and Aleck retired to their marriage chamber, leaving their guests to dance, sing and drink all night long if they wished. They were happy to bask in the glow of the love they now shared, knowing at least some of what the future had in store for them.

EPILOGUE

E DNA CAMPBELL COULDN'T help herself. She simply had to peek in to see how the Sinclair's were doing. She hadn't much to do with their match, but she loved a good romance and wasn't ashamed to be nosy. She was, after all, a self-proclaimed meddler in the love lives of some of her favorite couples. She made herself comfortable in front of her fire, where she had her tea and biscuits within easy reach. She took a few deep breaths, concentrating on the center of the hearth where the hottest embers popped and cracked. Before long she found herself completely engrossed in the scene she saw in the flames. To Edna this was on an equal par with reading a really good romance novel. Since Anania, too, was keeping an eye on the happy couple, she knew that things were going well at Sinclair Castle.

ISLA AND ALECK looked out over the great hall. No longer the solitary dining place of its laird, they had guests most nights and on the nights when they wished to be alone, the others enjoyed the bounty of the Sinclair kitchen in the hall and Aleck and Isla took their meal in their chambers.

On this night, they joined their guests. Aleck's men had been invited to come for the evening meal every night if they wished and to bring their families along with them. They were surrounded by the happy sounds of people enjoying each other's company and it gave them both a sense of family. A very large family to be sure, but one that they both wanted and one they would be adding to in the near future.

Aleck raised his wine in a private toast to his wife. "Isla, ye've given me more than I could have ever hoped. I wanted ye for a wife and I've gotten that and more. Ye are the reason I wake up in the morning. The reason I have hope for the future and I can hardly wait until we have all those bairns we've been promised by Dylan's family tree."

Isla gazed at him with a love he'd longed for, but wasn't sure he deserved. She touched his cheek with her hand and gazed at him with deep brown eyes that always drew him in to their warmth. "I'm happy, Aleck. Happier than I believed I could ever be. I was a fool to think that denying meself love and a home of my own would give me peace. I havenae known true peace until now, with ye. I love ye."

He dipped his head and gently kissed her lips. The crowd around them hushed and they both looked up to see everyone watching them. They laughed and the others joined in.

"Go back to yer meals," Aleck commanded.

Many in the crowd raised their mugs of ale to salute them and shouted their good wishes for the happy couple before returning to their own conversations.

"When do ye think we'll have our first bairn?" he asked.

"Sooner than ye think." Her eyes twinkled with merriment.

"Nae." Aleck couldn't believe his ears.

"Aye." She laughed.

He stood and scooped her up out of the chair and into his arms. Then thinking he might be squeezing her too hard set her back down. "I'm sorry. I didnae think. I dinnae wish to hurt the bairn."

"Aleck, I'm sturdier than ye think and so is our babe."

"I want to tell everyone." He was about to speak when Isla interrupted him.

"Let's keep it our wee secret for now, love. There's much time to tell them."

He pressed his forehead to hers and counted himself the luckiest man on earth.

A NOTE FROM JENNAE

THANK YOU so much for reading Her Noble Highlander. If you enjoyed the book and have a minute to spare, I would really appreciate it if you would leave a short review on the page or site where you bought the book. Your help in spreading the word is greatly appreciated. Reviews from readers like you make a huge difference in helping new readers find stories similar to Her Noble Highlander.

If you'd like to know when my next book comes out and want to receive occasional updates from me, then you can sign up for my newsletter here http://www.jennaevaleauthor.com/news-and-events

You can also follow me on BookBub here https://www.bookbub.com/authors/jennae-vale and GoodReads here https://www.goodreads.com/author/show/8634278.Jennae_Vale

ACKNOWLEDGMENTS

THERE ARE MANY components to writing a book and I'm grateful to the people who've helped me with it. Thank you to Sheri L. McGathy for her amazing cover design, to Jen Greybeal for her editing skills, and as always, a big thank you to my famiy and friends for your support.

ABOUT THE AUTHOR

JENNAE VALE IS a best selling author of romance with a touch of magic. As a history buff from an early age, Jennae often found herself day-dreaming in history class - wondering what it would be like to live in the places and time periods she was learning about. Writing time travel romance has given her an opportunity to take those daydreams and turn them into stories to share with readers everywhere.

Originally from the Boston area, Jennae now lives in the San Francisco Bay area, where some of her characters also reside. When Jennae isn't writing, she enjoys spending time with her family and her pets, and daydreaming, of course.

Connect with Jennae
www.jennaevaleauthor.com
jennaevaleauthor@gmail.com

www.ingramcontent.com/pod-product-compliance
Lightning Source LLC
Chambersburg PA
CBHW060218180626
46813CB00007B/2868